James Spilling

Me and Mine

James Spilling

Me and Mine

ISBN/EAN: 9783744790567

Printed in Europe, USA, Canada, Australia, Japan

Cover: Foto ©Andreas Hilbeck / pixelio.de

More available books at **www.hansebooks.com**

ME AND MINE

ME AND MINE

BY

JAMES SPILLING

AUTHOR OF "THE RVENING AND THE MORNING," ETC.

"These limbs, whence had we them; this stormy
force; this life-blood with its burning passion? They
are dust and shadow; a shadow system gathered
around our ME."

—CARLYLE's *Sartor Resartus.*

JAMES SPEIRS

36 BLOOMSBURY STREET, LONDON

1884

INTRODUCTION.

——o——

THE Author has in this work endeavoured to explain and illustrate the correlation between the Soul and the Body. To enforce his conclusions he has cited innumerable passages from the Sacred Scriptures. Fancies could not surely be sustained by so many Facts. The main aim of the Author has been to show the reality and substantiality of the Soul and the Spiritual World, and that the Body and the Natural World are comparatively shadowy and unreal. The highest modern literature is full of this truth; but men fail either to discern or believe it even while reading and admiring the works in which it is taught. Spenser, Shakspere, Milton, Coleridge, Wordsworth, and Goethe have all recognised and expressed this truth in fragments. Emerson teaches it out straight. Carlyle asserts it in *Sartor Resartus* from beginning to end. Mr. and Mrs. Browning have made the century melodious with it. Tennyson repeatedly enshrines the thought in his poetry. Even Shelley had a glimpse of it. How is it, then, that while these authors are read and admired the truth they teach is accepted by so few? I suppose the generalities of the poets and essayists escape notice. The fact is, the religion of the age is mainly materialistic. Existence in heaven even is held to be imperfect without the material resurrection. The votaries of such a faith are unprepared to believe that anything is substance except matter. They are more sceptical than the Sceptics. Spirit is with them less than mist and vapour; but "whether they will hear or whether they will forbear," our duty is plain, and therefore the following pages have been written.

CONTENTS.

CORRESPONDENCES.

INTERLUDES.

Me and Mine.

PRELUDE.

OUR PARTY.

THE summer morning is calm and sweet. The air is soft, but fresh with the smell of ocean. A mild light lies upon the brisk waves, which roll up with a murmurous sound, and break and dash upon the beach. The friends who are seated on the shingle, just beyond the reach of the advancing tide, are the members of two families bound together by congeniality of feeling rather than similarity of opinion, their differences only serving as salt to season their affection. Indeed, they are as divergent in their views of nature, life, and religion as they can very well be. Those of my readers who have patience to listen to them will learn more about them than any description can convey. I will, however, briefly introduce them before they are allowed to speak.

Mr. Rivers is a man of mature years. He is a thoughtful student of Nature and the Word of God. His views are settled and his convictions strong. He has, however, a comprehensive charity, which regards with respect the opinions of all classes of his fellow-creatures.

A

He knows by experience with what sincerity error may be received as truth. His own way was beset with thorns and briers, and through them he had to push and break into an open place and a plain path. Beset in early life by Doubts, he fought through the phalanx of his foes and won his way to Faith. Mr. Hawthorne, on the contrary, began in Faith and ended in Doubt. He is a humane man, and is pained at thought of the suffering creation. The disorders in the world and the disparities in society have affected his reason and warped his judgment. Moreover, his conclusions have been confirmed by the theories of the scientists. He wants to see heaven realized on earth, and every one placed in a rose-paradise without having to struggle through a wilderness to reach it. In short, he has those profound half views of things which constitute scepticism. Edith Hawthorne, a bright, intelligent girl of twenty, retains a belief, notwithstanding her father's influence, in the routine orthodox faith with which she had been indoctrinated at school. No difficulties disturb the serene depths of her mind. Faith is a clear, calm lake—very shallow—in the centre of her soul, and reason has never yet dropped one single pebble into it to cause a ripple upon its surface. She never has reasoned, and she thinks she never will reason, on the subject of religion. It is her duty to believe, and believe she will, in spite of her father's scepticism or Mr. Rivers' heterodoxical opinions. She holds that the only form of literature suitable for the sea-side is the novel, and a light specimen of it she is assiduously reading this August morning. George Rivers, who is sitting by her side, sympathizes with his father's views, although he has not specially studied them. He is a reader of every kind of useful and ornamental literature, but especially is he a student of the poets. He is now resting his head upon a pile of what Edith is pleased to call "frowsy bards," strapped together, but ready for use, to wile away the minutes between conversation, and to relieve his eyes when tired of gazing upon the sea. He holds somewhat loosely, gathered from a variety of books, similar ideas to those which are bound in a compact system in his father's mind. Mrs. Rivers, quiet, taciturn, and motherly, listens with deference to her husband, whose views she accepts without hesitation, and wonders how any one can be found to dispute them.

This is our party ; this the time; these the surroundings. Genial souls. The soft summer. Before, the ocean, a heaving mass of light and sound ; behind, the earth green and beautiful, with hills and vales, trees and flowers. Above, the great golden eye gazing calmly from its cloud bower of azure and silver light. What a scene for our actors to embellish, in which to speak their speech and play their part !

At a pause in the conversation George Rivers raised his head from off his pile of books, and was about to unbind the strap to withdraw a volume, when his eyes were arrested by the stirring scene.

CHAPTER I.

SUBSTANCE AND SHADOW.

George : What a vision of beauty! Did you, Mr. Hawthorne, ever witness a finer sight? What a picture! The ships out yonder with their white and swelling sails, and the steamers that walk the waters by a living invisible force as if there were a heart throbbing within their frame! What a divine blue, too, spreads over our heads and gazes down into its own beauty mirrored in the ocean!

Edith (looking up from her reading) : Whom are you quoting, George? Is that from the Laureate's last?

George : It's original, Edith, and I'll turn it for you into blank verse. Have you no soul for this mighty epic of Nature? Hark, what music!

> " The lightning of the noontide ocean
>   Is flashing round me, and a tone
>   Arises from its measured motion :
> How sweet did any heart now share in my emotion !"

Edith : Ha! ha! That's real poetry with rhymes to it. "Any heart," indeed! Whose would you like it to be?

George: Yours, Edith; but I fancy by the look of your volume that "Ouida" has it at the present moment.

Mr. Hawthorne (interposing): Well, I participate in your admiration, George, if I don't share in your emotion. Nature is to me ever new and ever wonderful. It is a book of glories and mysteries unfathomable. But, after all, it's a great enigma.

George: To be unriddled by and by.

Edith: That's Tennyson.

Hawthorne: I don't know, George. The world with all its beauty is a theatre of as much woe as joy, of as much pain as pleasure. If there's a "by and by," He who made this made that, and I fear both will be alike.

Mr. Rivers: You find the book of Nature an enigma, and therefore, you see, another book is required to explain it.

Hawthorne: Truly; but where is the explanatory volume, and who can open it?

Rivers: Nature is explicable by Spirit. The key to the natural world is the spiritual world. What can explain this body of ours but the spirit? Who can understand heart, lungs, hand, foot, eyes, ears, nose, and mouth, without the living spirit? They are useless in the corpse. But when you find a living man behind them all, perceiving and acting with them, they are easily explicable.

Hawthorne: Ah, yes; I perceive your meaning, but I differ from you respecting the fact of life. What is spirit? Vague, unsubstantial shadow! Nature we know. Nature is substance. Spirit we do not know. It is the mist of imagination—a shade conjured up by human thought.

George : The best minds of the age are against you, Mr. Hawthorne.

Edith : Pray define for us in our ignorance what the "best minds" of the age are.

George : Those of the poets, pussy, whom your novelists think so much of, seeing that they choose their best bits to put at the heads of their chapters. Even your own poet, Mr. Hawthorne, even Shelley saw that spirit is more real and substantial than matter.

Hawthorne : Indeed. I can scarcely believe it.

George : Oh yes! He says—

> " How glorious art thou, Earth. And if thou be
> The *shadow* of some *spirit* lovelier still."

You see he puts earth as shadow, and spirit as the lovelier substance thereof.

Edith : What Christian cares what Shelley said, I should like to know?

Hawthorne : Better and wiser than many Christians, Edith.

Rivers : We have touched an important theme, but very lightly. I think, with George, that real things are those of the spiritual world, and shadowy things those of the natural world. The sun up there is a mighty fire; but what is that when compared with that vaster fire, God's all-blazing love? The natural sun, with all its light and heat, is but the shadow of the spiritual sun, in the midst of which God's love burns. What is this earth? A rolling ball of matter diversified with hill and valley, tree and flower, beast and man, and lighted up by the lamp of day. This dwelling-place of the natural man is but the shadow of the dwelling-place of the spiritual man, which is lighted by the Lord God Almighty.

George : Earth is the shadow of heaven, and a very blotched one. Nature is the simulation of spirit. That is what Browning tells us—

> "There is
> Heaven, since there is Heaven's simulation, Earth."

That is like pointing to the shadowy simulation of a man upon these sands, and arguing thence the existence of the man.

Hawthorne : Come, come. No sensible person can believe in such notions as these. The dreams of poets and the conclusions of practical men are not to be placed in the same category.

Rivers : Many practical men believe in such notions. That the earth revolves round the sun was once a dream, but it is now the fact of practical men. But I recur to my first thought, that Nature is only explicable by Spirit. Can you explain a picture, statue, poem, without the mind of the artist? Is a man's work real, and his thought that produced it non-real? Nay, is not the mind substance, and its projection or work its shadow?

Hawthorne : Well, if you choose to consider it so, I have no objection. I care not, however, for terms; I rely on facts. The rock that kills a man is substance, and the mind that the rock dissipates is the mere exhalation of brain, and in comparison with the rock mere shadow.

Rivers : That is a strong assertion. It is a statement that has to be tested. What do you mean by a rock killing a man? Can a rock *do* anything? I thought action came from life.

George: Mr. Hawthorne means that one man may kill another with a piece of rock. In that case it is life acting upon life. The rock is nothing more than what a living force makes of it. As Coleridge says in relation to our impressions derived from the natural world—

> " We receive but what we give,
> And in *our* life alone does *nature* live."

Hawthorne: Your poets are too subtle for me, George. I referred to the rock which falls of itself from the mountain upon the traveller below. In that case the solid substance destroys life, dissipates your mental mist, let your poets and religionists say what they may.

Rivers: Not so. Rock can only affect rock, or matter that is of the nature of rock. Falling from a mountain, a stone may crush a man's body; but his thought, his love! Can it touch that? Could a piece of rock crush your love for Edith out of your brain?

Edith: Nonsense, Mr. Rivers; father doesn't believe anything so silly.

Hawthorne: But I believe, Edith, that a piece of rock can crush the life out of the body. That's common knowledge and common sense.

Rivers: Yes. A piece of rock can crush, as I have said, that which is of its own nature, the body, and make it unfit for the home of the soul. It can crush *out* the life; but you said it could *destroy* the life. How can a dead thing destroy a living thing? You despise poetry and ask for logic. Let us have it.

Hawthorne: Doesn't a dead cannon-ball destroy a living man?·

Rivers: Certainly not. A living man is a loving, thinking subject. What relation has a dead cannon-ball to life, love, thought? Say that it can mutilate the flesh and spill the blood. What then? You have yet to show that life is mutilated and love and thought spilled by a cannon-ball.

Hawthorne: Well, if you put things in that way, there is no getting on with an argument. You make as many assumptions as I do. You assume that life is independent of matter, which is contrary to our everyday experience.

Rivers: I say that life is *above* matter—moulds it, qualifies it, is the substance of it. Let us take your own theory. What is now earth was once a fire mist, without life. It cooled down, and became rock, water, soil. The dead matter was all of the same dead character. At length life was breathed into it, and straightway there is vegetable body and animal body. What are those bodies but the visible shadowings forth of the invisible substantiality life, moulding it, and in its own form making tree, fish, bird, reptile, quadruped, man? Did dead earth make man or a living force? Now, if all the things on earth are the shadows of living forces, then those forces must be substances revealing themselves in Nature. Thus, as George has said, Earth is the shadow of Heaven.

George: Milton suggests the same thing, as you know—

" What if earth
Be but the shadow of heaven, and things therein,
Each to other like, more than on earth is thought?"

Earth and all the things upon the earth are the shadows of living substances.

Rivers: Now, my dear Hawthorne, you know that a shadow corresponds with its substance. The shadow corresponds with the tree, the reflection in the mirror with the object reflected. What a wonderful study, therefore, would be that of Correspondences!

Edith: Oh, Mr. Rivers, that's the old story. If you begin on that I may as well shut my book, or go and sit under the boat there all alone, for there'll be no peace. I never have understood it, and never shall, and never will.

Mrs. Rivers: Don't say so, Edith. I thought so once. Put up your book for this morning, and let us all try to learn something.

Hawthorne: I am surprised at you, Edith. What is life for, if it is not to teach and to learn?

George: Oh, Mr. Hawthorne, life is in eternity like a green oasis in a desert, where you can lie under a shady tree, and soothe yourself with novels and romances till the night comes down, and then—then—a gentle sleep!

Edith: Or, perhaps, life is an opportunity to spell over a host of frowsy poets, and get credit by pretending to understand them. If *I* can't read, neither shall you, George. Pack up that old Wordsworth you are fingering there, and let us all look wondrous wise, and listen to our seniors. Now, Mr. Rivers, correspondences; for the hundredth time let us hear all about them. Analogies, emblems, symbols, types, are they not? Just the things for youthful poets made.

CHAPTER II.

CORRESPONDENCES.

Rivers: Well, Edith, since you ask me, I must tell you that analogies, emblems, symbols, or types, are not correspondences.

Edith: What is the difference? I have heard you talk about the sun meaning this and the moon meaning that, and if they are not emblems I cannot understand you.

Rivers: Correspondences are founded on the correlation of things natural with things spiritual. Thus a visible natural object, which is an effect, corresponds with the invisible spiritual force which is its cause. That is not so with analogies and emblems. An analogy is a likeness or similarity between two natural objects having no relationship of cause and effect. Thus, there is an analogy between a fish and a bird, because the one propels itself through the water by fins and the other through the air by wings. Again, a plant is analogous to an animal, because both have life and grow. Emblems and symbols mean pretty well the same, the words having a similar derivation. They are arbitrary or poetic representations of one thing by another. For instance, a woman blindfolded having a pair of scales in her hand is an emblem or symbol of justice. A white rose was the emblem or symbol of the house of York, and a red rose of Lancaster. Now a fish does not correspond to a bird, a plant to an animal, a blindfolded woman to justice, nor a rose to any party.

Edith : But I am sure correspondences are types, Mr. Rivers.

George : Don't be sure of anything in this uncertain world, Edith.

Edith : Not even, I suppose, that poetry and pertness both begin with the same letter.

Rivers : Types are used in the Scriptures, but they are not correspondences. Thus, David was a type of the Lord, not the correspondence. He was the representative of the Lord. Correspondences are, I say again, the relationships which exist between things spiritual and things natural.

Hawthorne : Ah! there you are again. You are assuming the existence of things spiritual before proving it.

Rivers : Well, well, let us then understand one another as we go along. We admit the existence of natural things. Will you define them ?

Hawthorne : Natural things are whatever come within the range of our senses. Whatever we can see, hear, smell, taste, or touch. Yon glowing sun, this heaving ocean, these shining pebbles, this bracing air, the blue firmament—these are Nature.

George : Ah, these are what Goethe calls "the mantle of God." The mantle or garment has somewhat of a correspondence with the body, the shoes with the feet, the hat with the head, the trousers with the limbs, the

coat with the back. Now, God is a spirit, and if Nature
is His garment, see how Spirit and Nature correspond.

Edith : Where did you learn all that, George?

George : From Gœthe, in *Faust.* Don't you know
the lines? The earth-spirit sings :

> "At the whirring loom of Time, unawed
> I work the living mantle of God."

Just think of that! All nature is the woven garment of
God.

Edith : Dear me, how learned we are !

Rivers : My dear Hawthorne, I admit the accuracy of
your definition. Nature is whatever comes within the
range of the senses. Now I suppose you accept the
existence of Affection and Thought? You yourself love
and think. Can you see or hear an affection? Can you
taste or touch a thought?

Hawthorne : Of course not. But I don't call affections
and thoughts "things." They are mere fancies, or
imaginations, or emanations from the brain.

Rivers : Oh! Is your love for your child a fancy, an
imagination, an emanation from your brain? Is it less
real than this speck of foam now melting on your hand?
Is the thought that moulds the statue less real than the
marble that it chooses and chisels? Affection and
thought are the forces that use the dead things of
nature. Are the objects used "things," and the forces
that use not "things"?

Hawthorne : They are not things that can be taken
cognisance of by the senses.

Rivers : No; for they are above nature. They are not
to be seen, heard, smelt, tasted, or touched. But they

can be brought into nature. Affection and thought can be brought into the realm of sense. For instance: you speak your love and thought, and bring it into the atmosphere of nature, so that I *hear* it. You write, and bring your love and thought into the light of nature, so that I *see* it. Again, you express your love and thought in a modelled image, and reveal it in the *matter* of nature, so that I *touch* it. Now, in all these cases, can you not see how the things brought into nature—the speech, the written sentence, and the modelled image—are related to that which produced them, and which, being love and thought, I call spiritual?

Hawthorne : Well, I can see that there must be a relationship between our thoughts and our words or deeds.

Rivers : That relationship I call correspondence.

Hawthorne : Then I admit that there is a correspondence between what I *think* and what I *say, write*, or *make*. If you call the thought spiritual and the speech natural, I concede the point.

Rivers : But I cannot do otherwise than call the one spiritual and the other natural. Think of your own definition : that which is natural is what can be heard. You cannot hear a thought till it breaks into speech. The word which you hear is natural, and the corresponding thought within it is spiritual. Now as one utterance corresponds with one thought, so a great number of utterances correspond with a succession of thoughts. Every book corresponds with the extended and continuous thought of its author. We speak of the book of Nature. Nature is a book expressive of the Divine Mind, and every object in Nature is like a sentence in a book, corresponding with the love and wisdom which formed it. As a printed volume corresponds with the mind of its human author, so the universe corresponds with the Mind of God.

Hawthorne : The idea is fine, like George's poetical illustrations. So far I can go with you. But we draw a wide distinction between Science, which is fact, and Poetry, which is imagination.

Rivers : But I am asking you to take a scientific and not an imaginative view of our subject. It is positive fact that every word is the outbirth, and therefore the effect and correspondence, of some thought, and thus that every object in Nature is the outbirth of some Divine perception respecting its use. For instance, as you say, there is the sun. Do you think it came into existence without some reference to its use in the universe ? I might as well ask you whether a printing machine came into existence without any regard to its use in society. Does not the sun mean heat, light, and life in the world, just as the printing machine means printed sheets and the diffusion of intelligence among the people? The sun, therefore, corresponds with the perception of its use in the mind of its Creator. It corresponds with that Love and Wisdom which discerned its need and produced it. This is science, not imagination.

Hawthorne : At present I don't see exactly what you are coming to.

Rivers : No. Let us therefore go a little further. We enter an artist's studio, and find ourselves surrounded with specimens of his skill. Here is the model of a lovely female head, and there is the statue of a grotesque. These things evidently represent different phases of the artist's mind, and correspond with those phases. Transfer the thought to Nature. Nature is the studio of the

Divine Artist. It is filled with specimens of His skill—
men and women; beasts, birds, and fishes; mountains
and valleys; seas and rivers; sun, moon, and stars. All
these represent Wisdom in its various degrees and phases
as it flows from the Divine Mind, and correspond with it.

Edith: And yet you said that correspondences were,
not emblems, Mr. Rivers. Now you say that sun, moon,
and stars represent wisdom in its various phases. How
can they represent what they are not emblems of?

George: It seems ladies in these days are critical if
they are not poetical !

Rivers: While emblems ·are not correspondences,
Edith, correspondences may be emblems. An eagle is
the emblem of France, a lion of England; but the eagle
and the lion are not correspondences of those countries.
The sun is the correspondence of Divine Love because
love warms the soul, and the moon of Divine Truth,
because truth enlightens the soul. Being correspondences, you may, if you like, also call them emblems.

George: Words correspond with thoughts because they
originate in thoughts. The objects in nature are God's
words, and therefore they correspond with His thought.
The universe is God's book. Just listen, Edith—

> " The world's no blot for us
> Nor blank—it means intensely, and means good."

If you want to know what it means you must master the
Alphabet of Nature, which consists of correspondences.

Edith: Thanks for the advice; but with so wise an
interpreter close at hand there is no need to take the
trouble.

Rivers: Hush, you young ones. I take George's

thought, that the objects of nature are God's words. Now what God meant by sun, moon, and stars in the universe He means in the Bible. The sun means, as I have said, heat, life, light, and unbounded influence in the material world. In the Bible the sun means heat, life, light, and unbounded influence in the spiritual world of our souls. For instance, "Thy sun shall no more go down, . . . for the Lord shall be thine everlasting light." Our sun, which is not to go down, is the Lord Himself, who fills our spirits with spiritual heat, which is love ; with spiritual light, which is intelligence ; with spiritual life, which is virtue ; with spiritual influence, which guides all our goings forth. Thus the sun corresponds with all these things, because from its natural uses it represents spiritual uses. In other words, the use which the sun serves to the body, the Lord, the Divine Sun, serves to the soul. So it is with all things. The objects in nature correspond with the forces in the soul. If you would understand the Bible aright you must understand something of the science of correspondences.

Hawthorne: Science? Why, science is exact knowledge. You can have nothing of the kind in such metaphysical excursions as you are now making.

Rivers: Science is knowledge, and knowledge grows. The science of astronomy in its infancy was very imperfect. But the law of the stars was the same then as now. So in our case. The law of correspondences is fixed and certain. Our knowledge of the science is imperfect. But it will grow. To the extent to which we understand it the Bible is a new book.

Hawthorne: Well, I should certainly like to see the transformation. I am afraid, however, that I should be

B

no better off than Aladdin, whose new lamp was not worth his old one.

Rivers: We shall see.

Edith: Oh, here is Jane with luncheon !

George: Ah ! now we shall see what an appetite is ! I will add a line to my last quotation :

> "To find its meaning is my meat and drink."

Edith: Meaning? Of what—an appetite?

George: No, no; of this wondrous world, which is "no blot for us nor blank," but "means intensely, and means good."

INTERLUDE I.

"WHAT SHALL WE EAT?"

EDITH was too busy in unrolling the parcel of sandwiches, biscuits, and buttered rusks to pay any attention to the last sly sally, and presently the friends were in voluble discourse on the excellence of the provisions supplied them by their landlady.

"A splendid thing for an appetite is a mouthful of sea-air," said George, despatching his third sandwich.

"Bless me," said Edith, "I wonder you didn't bring down a cookery book instead of that batch of bards; your studies might then have been improving for all of us."

"My batch of bards would unfold to you more about the virtues and beauties of a good luncheon than you are aware of, my dear," said George, laughing.

"Oh, I thought they lived off sunbeams and the breath of eglantines," said Edith.

"Certainly not," said George; "blackbirds baked in a pie, and when the pie is opened the birds begin to sing, and imitate the tuneful brotherhood. But now, to give you the picture of a luncheon better than you will find in any cookery book:

> '' There on a slope of orchard, Francis laid
> A damask napkin wrought with horse and hound,
> Brought out a dusky loaf that smelt of home,
> And, half-cut down, a pasty costly-made,¹
> Where quail and pigeon, lark and leveret lay,
> Like fossils of the rock, with golden yolks
> Imbedded and injellied.'

Wouldn't you have liked a bit?"

"And does the bard—sweet sympathetic soul—tell us who killed the quails and pigeons, the larks and the leverets?" said Edith, with an air of mock seriousness; "were they killed with a common, vulgar, prosaic gun?"

"I am glad you have asked the question, Edith," said Mr. Rivers; "as you see, I eat only my biscuit and buttered rusk. The flesh of once living things I avoid. I cannot think our Heavenly Father ever intended that before we could get a breakfast we should go and kill a beautiful creature and get out its kidney to grill."

"Oh, horrid!" shrieked Edith.

"You didn't do it yourself this morning," said Rivers, "but you had to get somebody to do it for you, Edith. Now how much better did they feast in Paradise! Have we not a finer picture of a banquet there than the one you have just given us, George?"

"That depends upon tastes," said George, laughing again; "this is how Adam and the angel fared in Eden with Eve:

> ' Fruit of all kinds, in coat
> Rough, or smooth rind, or bearded husk, or shell,
> She gathers; tribute large! and on the board
> Heaps with unsparing hand; for drink the grape
> She crushes, inoffensive must, and meathes
> From many a berry; and from sweet kernels pressed
> She tempers dulcet creams.'

It was very nice, and would· have been capital after a mutton-chop, or the quail and pigeon, lark and leveret pie."

"But, my dear Rivers," said Hawthorne, "do you really believe it to be wrong to feed on the flesh of animals ? "

"I do," said Rivers; "the Divine ordinance was, 'The herb bearing seed, and the fruit-tree yielding seed, to you it shall be for meat.'"

"But God, according to the Bible, gave all sorts of directions about slaughtering animals and eating their flesh," said Hawthorne.

"The first instructions," said Rivers, "had relation to the eating of herbs and fruits. That was when man was in a state of innocence. When men became corrupt, and made war upon each other and upon the inferior races, then God *permitted* the eating of flesh. It was in the case of food as in the case of wives. For the hardness of their hearts Moses wrote for the Jews the precept respecting the putting away of their wives; 'but,' said the Lord, 'in ·the beginning it was not so.' The same principle is applicable to our diet. For the hardness of men's hearts God permitted flesh-eating, but in the beginning it was not so."

"But if I remember rightly," urged Hawthorne, "the Lord Himself was a feeder on flesh. At any rate, He ate a bit of broiled fish."

"I am quite willing to give you what advantage that passage supplies, and also any argument that can be urged in the same direction from Abraham having entertained three angels with kneaded cakes and the flesh of a calf tender and good, as we read in Genesis. It was the Lord in His Divine resurrection body—which had no materiality about it, as it appeared in the midst of the disciples in a closed room—who ate the fish; and they were heavenly beings who are said to have eaten the carnal earthly food with Abraham. The passages require interpretation. However, they certainly teach that God sanctions the eating of flesh and fish to those who can do it conscientiously. I cannot."

"But, Rivers, do not physiologists assert that we are designed by nature to feed on flesh? Have we not canine teeth?"

"If we were designed by Nature to feed on flesh, the race would universally and invariably do so. But there are whole nations, comprising millions of people, who are vegetarians. Either they depart from nature in avoiding it, or others depart from nature in eating it. This fact shows that Nature has given no instructions on the subject. If we were taught by Nature, we should all be flesh-feeders or vegetarians. But we are left to our own course, according to education or predisposition."

"But how about the canine teeth, Mr. Rivers?" said Edith.

"Well, Edith, if there is any force in that argument, it means that if you wanted to feed on a hare you would seize it with your canine teeth as a dog does, and as a dog devour it. If it does not mean that, there is no sense in the argument."

"I am afraid reason is all on the side of father," said George; "and if reason is not, certainly sweetness and beauty are. Here is a picture by Shelley:

'Gore
Or poison none this festal did pollute;
But piled on high an overflowing store

Of pomegranates and citrons—fairest fruit,
Melons, and dates, and figs, and many a root
Sweet and sustaining, and bright grapes.'

But what is all that to the mouth that waters for a beef-steak?"

"I will give you my faith upon the subject in a very few words," said Mr. Rivers, taking a small scrap of paper from his pocket-book, and beginning to read: "'To eat the flesh of animals, considered in itself, is somewhat profane; for the people of the most ancient times never, on any account, ate the flesh of any beast or fowl, but fed solely on grain, especially on bread made of wheat, on the fruit of trees, herbs, milks of various kinds, and what is produced from them, as butter and so forth.'"

"Stop, stop! who is your author?" asked Hawthorne. " The men of the most ancient times certainly lived on flesh. The bones of animals which had been evidently eaten are found among those of the Cave Man of pre-historic days."

"I am speaking of the *most* ancient times," replied Rivers. "I believe the Cave Men were their degenerated descendants. Prior to everything that science professes to know of, I believe there were a people high and wise, and that they shrank from bloodshed. Will you hear the rest of my extract?"

"Oh, certainly."

"'To kill animals and eat their flesh was to them un-lawful, being regarded as something bestial; and they were content with the uses and services which animals yielded. But in the course of time, when mankind became cruel as the wild beasts—yea, much more cruel—they then first began to slay animals and eat their flesh;

and as man had acquired such a nature, therefore the killing and eating of animals was permitted and continues to be so to the present day.'"

"Well, well, that is comfortable at any rate," said Hawthorne; "but I asked you before, who's your author?"

"Swedenborg," said Rivers curtly.

"Ah, the man that, as Carlyle hints, made a leap to solve the universe and tumbled into bedlam," remarked Hawthorne, with a satirical smile.

"Or rather," said George, "the man whom Carlyle's clear-headed friend Emerson declares to be the *one* who, ' of all men in the recent ages, stands eminently for the translator of nature into thought.'"

"We won't dispute that subject," said Hawthorne.

"Hear the remainder of the piece respecting the eating of flesh," said Rivers, referring to his paper. "Here it is. 'Now, so far as man can do this conscientiously, it is lawful, for his conscience is formed of what he thinks to be true, consequently what he regards as lawful; wherefore also at this day no one is ever condemned for eating flesh.'"

"Then I may still have my grilled kidney for breakfast?" asked Edith, with a serio-comic look.

"So far as you can conscientiously set a butcher to kill and cut to pieces the beautiful timid creature," said George, with assumed severity.

"My dear," said Mrs. Rivers kindly, "we are permitted to act according to our consciences, and allowances are made for our weakness. We desire to bring Eden back to man, but while we destroy life to live we shall be more or less in a wilderness."

The little party had finished their mid-day meal, and rose from the sands and wandered along the beach. The subject on which they had been conversing gave place to a dozen others, nor was it renewed until they found themselves all together in their brightly illuminated sitting-room at the close of the day.

CHAPTER III.

MAN.

Hawthorne: Now, Rivers, for a renewal of the conversation we began this morning.

Rivers: With all my heart. The matter is easily understood. Visible effects correspond with invisible causes. Thus, Earth, which is an effect, corresponds with Heaven, which is a cause. For the same reason the Body corresponds with the Soul.

George: Spenser is with us there :—

> "For of the soul the bodie forme doth take,
> For soul is forme and doth the bodie make."

All bodies necessarily correspond with the soul that moulds and informs them.

Edith: Hear our young philosopher ! The chair has a body, and I suppose it is in the form of its soul.

George: What other form is possible ?

Hawthorne: Come, come, this is trifling.

Rivers: Not so, my dear Hawthorne. I am surprised at George's remark, but still I can support him. The chair *has* a soul, and it exists from the soul of its maker !

George: I wonder how many of the admirers of *Aurora Leigh* have understood these words—

"Natural things
And spiritual—who separates those two
In *art*, in morals, or the social drift,
Tears up the bond of nature, and brings death."

Every picture and every work of industry was first in the spiritual world of its author's mind. Our morals and our social habits are fixed by spiritual forces. Things of Art have such life as human souls can give; things of Nature such life as God bestows.

Rivers : But, not to go beyond nature, you will admit that a vegetable body corresponds with a vegetable soul, an animal body with an animal soul, and a human body with a human soul.

Hawthorne : A vegetable soul! This is the first time I have heard the phrase. Many of us doubt the existence of a human soul, and I fear your talk about a vegetable soul is only calculated to raise a smile.

Rivers : How could there be a vegetable body if there were no vegetable soul? A vegetable body is the effect of the operation of vegetable life. In the seed of the oak there is the soul of the oak, and if you put the seed in the ground the soul will work out a body of like character with itself. Is not that plain? Two seeds, both externally alike, will work out very different results in plant form, because the soul in each is different. The soul of the rose and the soul of the violet mould around themselves bodies corresponding with their respective natures.

• *Hawthorne :* Yes. That is true so far. If you call the living vegetative force in a seed a soul, I have no objection to the use of the word, though we always associate immateriality and immortality with souls.

Rivers : Of course we associate immateriality with souls, but not necessarily immortality. A soul may be immaterial though not immortal. The living force in a seed is not matter. It clothes itself with matter, and this external clothing corresponds with the internal life. Why is there a difference between a vegetable and an animal? Because each is built up by a different living force or soul. Why does one animal body come in the form of a cat and another in the form of a dog? Because a cat-like soul can only find satisfaction in a cat-like body, and a dog-like soul in a dog-like body. In both cases the souls have corresponding bodies. Why are there apes and men? Because there are ape souls and human souls. An ape soul could no more mould and clothe itself in a human body, than a mouse soul could mould and clothe itself in the body of an elephant. Souls and bodies are correlated as cause and effect, and they therefore, as I have said, correspond.

Hawthorne : Ah, I see. You are aiming a subtle shaft at Darwinism.

Rivers : The foible of the "learned," the folly of the age. It assumes either that souls can change their nature in their seeds, or that they can put themselves into bodies out of harmony and therefore out of correspondence with themselves—an absurdity too gross fitly to characterize.

George : "To every seed his own body." I take Paul before Darwin.

Edith : Dear me! Poet, philosopher, theologian! Presently we shall have a youthful divine.

Hawthorne : Hush, Edith!

Rivers : How would a lion gratify its wants if its body were like that of a buffalo? A lion is a combination of certain desires and appetites which we call a soul, and how can they be appeased without a body with claws and fangs? Souls and bodies, interior forces and exterior forms, must correspond in order that things may exist. Now man is human in soul and body. Let us consider him. What is man?

Edith : An ugly ill-tempered creature, with a bundle of ragged poets strapped to his back.

Mrs. Rivers (smiling): And what, then, is woman?

George : In the person of Edith, mother, woman is

> " Earth's flower
> It holds up to the softened gaze of God."

But we can improve Edith's definition of man from one of the despised family of bards : " What a piece of work is man ! how noble in reason ! how infinite in faculties ! in form and moving how express and admirable ! in action how like an angel ! in apprehension how like a god ! the beauty of the world ! the paragon of animals !"

Edith : Humph ! Shakespeare !

Rivers : That is doubtless a fine definition of man. But I think I can give you a better. In Jeremiah v. 1 we read : " Run ye to and fro through the streets of Jerusalem, and see now, and know, and seek in the broad places thereof, if ye can find a man, if there be any that executeth judgment, that seeketh the truth ; and I will pardon it." In the Divine definition a man is one that " executeth judgment," that " seeketh the truth." There were many persons at that time in Jerusalem bearing the outward forms of men, but what God required was one that bore the genuine inward form or quality that constitutes a genuine man.

George : The mind's the standard of the man, Edith.

Edith : Indeed !

Rivers : Neither Alexander nor Cæsar was the first or noblest of men. The first and noblest of men was Jesus Christ, because He not only executed judgment and sought truth, but He was Judgment and Truth itself. Jesus being the first and noblest of men, and at the same time the "express image of the Father"—indeed, so much so that He said "He that hath seen me hath seen the Father"—it follows that the Father is a man.

Edith : How is that, Mr. Rivers? Why, the Father is God.

Rivers : Yes, and God is Man. He is the Infinite Man, and we are finite copies of Him.

George : Of course, because we are said to be in His image and after His likeness.

Rivers : And what is an image and a likeness but a shadow of the real thing? As earth is a shadow of heaven, so we are shadows of God. Moreover, as a shadow corresponds with its substance, so man and earth correspond with God and heaven. The real truth of the matter, then, is this, God is the Infinite Love and Wisdom, and man is a finite reflection of that Love and Wisdom. There are God, heaven, and earth, and all are in correspondence. God is Love and Wisdom itself. Heaven is love and wisdom as received by the angelic or spiritual man. Earth is love and wisdom as received by the rudimental or natural man. All the things on earth correspond with men's states, as they are receptive of the Lord's love and wisdom. All the things in heaven correspond with angels' states, as they are receptive. Thus, all in heaven and all in earth are from God, and have their final cause and correspondence in Him.

Hawthorne: A very high and mighty doctrine. I should like to see it proved. You have introduced as facts things unproven—God and heaven. But let that be. You have talked about earth corresponding with the Divine Love and Wisdom as seen in man. How about the ravenous and ferocious beasts? Are they correspondences of Love and Wisdom?

Rivers: Certainly, as distorted and perverted by ravenous and ferocious men. If men were all perfectly receptive of God, so that the Divine influences were received in, and reflected from, orderly souls, all would be orderly in nature. If the Divine were received into an interior garden, it would go forth in the creation of an exterior garden. Being received among interior lions and wolves, it goes forth in the creation of corresponding creatures in the natural world. But I must apologise. I am going out of our proper range and theme. We were speaking of man as being an image and likeness of God. God being Love and Wisdom, a man is man when he is good and true. But there are two sorts of men mentioned in the Bible.

George: Yes, the good and the bad.

Rivers: No. I don't mean the two classes. The bad are not properly speaking men. The two sorts to which I refer are the two sexes—male men, and female men.

Edith (laughing): How very ridiculous. Female men!

George: Yes, Edith. Tennyson will tell you that "woman is the lesser man."

Rivers: Certainly. Female men are spoken of in

Genesis i. 27. In Genesis v. 1, 2, the name of both the male and female is said to be Adam, and Adam means man. The Scriptures teach us that "in the day when they were created," the name of *both* was called "Man," though afterwards the wife is called Eve. Now both male men and female men are images and likenesses of the Lord, but the male is more receptive of the Lord's Wisdom than of His Love, and the woman more of His Love than of His Wisdom.

George : Hear that, Edith. Sarcasm doesn't make a woman, but love !

Edith : And the foppery of learning doesn't make a man, but wisdom.

Rivers : The woman should be loving, and wise because she is loving ; the man should be wise, and loving because he is wise. Now let this complex creature Man be our subject. In him all things are united.

George : As Herbert sings—

> " He is in little all the sphere."

He tells us that all things of this life, and of the other life too, are united in man. Thus he says—

> " Man ties them *both* alone,
> And makes them one.
> With th' one hand touching heaven, with th' other, earth."

Is it not exquisite ?

Edith : Very !

Hawthorne : My dear Rivers, you must forgive her. You and I were once young. I approve your design. I have just a hazy idea of your correspondences, but I should be glad to have them carried more into details.

Rivers : Well, we will endeavour to do that in good time.

INTERLUDE II.

"WITH WHAT BODIES DO THEY COME?"

AT a break in the conversation Edith sprang to the piano, and George joined her, and presently the room was flooded with the strains of witching music. Mrs. Rivers got her work and drew closer to the lamps. Hawthorne and his friend walked to the window to get a breath of air. The moon had risen over the sea, and the light lay like a broad path of silver upon the waters. The scene was so attractive that they determined to walk down to the beach to enjoy the soft breeze and the glorious commingling of heaven and earth which the night revealed.

"Ah," said Hawthorne as they were pacing over the shingle, with the small ripple of the waves in their ears, "'there is no night there.' Is not that what is written? To my mind that will be a decided loss. All one day of blazing heat! But what is the use of talking of days and nights, of light and darkness, in a vague, unsubstantial world of spirits without bodies?"

Rivers pressed his friend's arm, as if he were more desirous of enjoying the solemn loveliness of the scene than of entering into any discussion of the subject which Hawthorne's words suggested.

C

"Look at the vessels out yonder," said he, "with their lamps reflected in the water, some moving onward with their spreading sails flashing in the moonlight."

"Ah, yes," replied Hawthorne, "the scene is indeed full of life and loveliness ; but 'there will be no more sea,' and the sparkling, briny sea, fresh and crisp, makes the glory of existence. No night, no sea, no bodies—it will be a strange state of being ! The theory won't do."

Rivers paused a moment, and feeling it was impossible to avoid the subject, he asked, "Who says there will be no bodies ? Have I not told you that our theory is that this moon is but the shadowy embodiment of the Divine Moon—the Moon that shall not 'withdraw itself'—that lights the heavenly regions ? The real Moon—God's All-kindling Light—that beautifies the twilight of the spiritual world, is more substantial than the shadowy moon of the natural world. So the real body in which the soul is clothed in the spiritual world is more substantial than the unreal perishing body with which the soul is clothed in the natural world. Why, do we not read of spirits having been seen with bodily forms ?"

"What, do you believe in ghosts ?" said Hawthorne.

"Is not literature full of such belief ?" said Rivers. "The Greeks and Romans believed in spirits. Every nation believes in spirits. The Bible expressly teaches us that spirits have bodily forms, which under certain conditions have been visible to men upon earth. Abraham, Jacob, and the prophets saw spiritual beings as men. At the resurrection the women saw two *men* in shining garments at the sepulchre. If they were seen as men, I suppose they must have had bodies."

"I suppose so," said Hawthorne, musing ; "but, you

know, to me the Bible is no authority. I want reason
—fact. I never saw a spirit. I don't know any one
who ever did. What is in the range of experience we
can believe, but not what is beyond it."

"Certainly we must have mental or sensible experience before we can believe anything. I should like to
enlarge your mental experience. To begin with, my
dear Hawthorne, remember that you have only material
organs, and that they cannot recognise immaterial
things. But immaterial things are not the less real,
because you have not yet a sense with which to detect
them. The spiritual world to spiritual organs is real
and substantial. The heavenly landscapes are fairer than
mind can conceive. There are there sun, moon, stars,
flowers and trees, falling waters, murmuring brooks, and
all that can delight the elevated, refined, and purified
senses of the angels. But you must dismiss all thoughts
of materiality."

The two friends paused for a moment, looked across
the sea, and after a moment's silence began to retrace
their steps, when Hawthorne resumed the dialogue.

CHAPTER IV.

Hawthorne: And if after death bodies are not material, —which it is idle to suppose,—of what are they composed?

Rivers: I have told you; but it appears the idea is so strange that I must repeat myself—of SUBSTANCE.

Hawthorne: Well, but I cannot think of substance apart from matter.

Rivers: According to my theory, matter is to true substance only as its shadow. Is not God—supposing Him to exist—substance? Is not an angel—supposing there are such beings as angels—substance? Nothing exists but substance. There are two sorts of bodies— two sorts of substances. There are bodies terrestrial and there are bodies celestial. Are not celestial bodies substances? There are material or natural substances, and there are immaterial or spiritual substances. The material body, composed of natural substances, is constantly undergoing change, and at death it decomposes, and ultimately passès away and is gone like a shadow. The spiritual body, composed of immaterial substances, survives the natural body, and abides for ever.

Hawthorne: Yes, yes; that is very well as a theory. But we can see and handle the natural body. We know that it is composed of flesh and blood and bones. Here it is, occupying so much space. We can weigh it and measure it and test its reality. You can do nothing of the sort with what you are pleased to call a spiritual or immaterial body.

Rivers: True, I could not tell you the weight of your mind in pounds avoirdupois. But you know some men's minds are light as air, others have a surpassing gravity.

Hawthorne: Ah! there you are again: you always turn things off in that strange manner.

Rivers: The natural body is composed of Flesh, Blood, and Bone; and the spiritual body, of Goodness, Truth, and the sound solid Doctrine which they clothe. You can weigh Flesh in human scales; but Goodness is weighed in the Divine balances. Weigh the goodness and truth of a true Christian with that of a drunkard and a gambler. Which, think you, is the lightest? There are hardness and solidity about the Bones by which the physical frame is kept straight; but how much more solid and impenetrable is the Life-Doctrine of a true man which keeps his spiritual frame erect!

Hawthorne: But those are only ideas.

Rivers: Only ideas! Why, what is your *notion* about the weight of matter but an *idea!* But we are beating the wind. The spiritual body is a real body. It is more real than decaying flesh and blood and rotting bones. It is composed of that which is everlasting—Goodness and Truth. Goodness is real: Truth is real. Goodness is substance: Truth is substance. Goodness and Truth can be seen by the mental eye, grasped by the mental hand, weighed in the Divine scales, and measured by the heavenly rule. Goodness and Truth are to the spiritual body what Flesh and Blood are to the natural body. Hence Jesus said, " Except ye eat the flesh of the Son of man, and drink His blood, ye have no life in you."

Hawthorne : That was merely a figure of speech.

Rivers : True, but grounded in correspondences. The earthly body is the dark shadow of and corresponds with the heavenly body. The earthly body is composed of earthly substances, and the heavenly body of heavenly substances. The Lord's flesh that we can eat is the heavenly substance of Goodness, which, received and appropriated in the human spirit, gives us spiritual vitality and strength. The Lord's blood which we drink is the heavenly wine Truth, which, imbibed into the understanding, gives it freshness and exhilaration. I say that you have in this a striking illustration of the great law of correspondences. To eat and drink Christ is to open the soul to the reception of His Love and Wisdom, which are only other words for Goodness and Truth.

Hawthorne : Eat goodness! drink truth! You are talking in a strange language. I cannot comprehend it.

Rivers : I am talking in the language of correspondences, which is that of the Bible. Nay, it is the language of all literature, and even of everyday life. Do we not say that *minds* grow ? How could they grow unless they were *fed?* Bodies grow because they eat and drink natural things ; minds grow because they eat and drink spiritual things. If George were here he would show you how full literature is of the same language. I can now give you only one instance :—

" I say, that as the babe you feed awhile
    Becomes a boy, and fit to feed himself,
    So *minds* at first must be *spoon-fed* with Truth ;
    When they can *eat*, babes' nurture is withdrawn."

Every one understands that. Goodness and truth must be carefully prepared for infantile minds.

Hawthorne: But do you mean to tell me that the term " flesh " in the Bible can always be translated into the term " goodness," as you put it ?

Rivers : Yes ; because they correspond. The term flesh always means Goodness in the Scriptures. It means Goodness as it is in the eye of God, or Goodness as it is in the eye of the Devil. The latter goodness is evil, as Milton makes Satan exclaim, " Evil, be thou my good." In plain terms, flesh stands for goodness or its opposite, evil. I think you have seen that, when the Lord tells us that we must eat His flesh, He means that we must receive and appropriate His Goodness. Again, He says, " My flesh is meat indeed," and, " He who eateth my flesh hath eternal life." I know, Hawthorne, you are not so foolish as to imagine that Jesus spoke at random, or that He uttered idle words, having Himself told us that we must give account of such things in the day of judgment. If He did not utter idle words, what He said must have a meaning ; and I ask you whether it is not in accordance with sound judgment to conclude that He, being the Word made Flesh, spoke of the substance of His Divine Goodness, and which, being His Divine Body, must become incorporated in our spiritual bodies if we would have everlasting life ?

Hawthorne: The suggestion is feasible. But I cannot grasp the idea of a *body* being composed of *goodness*.

Rivers : No. The perception of such things only comes with time and study. A man really is what his Goodness makes him to be. He is not merely his body of flesh !

Hawthorne : True. That I can see.

Rivers : Well, you with your natural eyes look upon the body of flesh : an angel with his spiritual eyes looks not upon the body of flesh, but the body of goodness, which a man possesses. What is apparent to you is not apparent to the angel, and what is apparent to the angel is not apparent to you. If you had the spiritual sight of an angel you would not see the form of my flesh, but the form of my goodness ; and it would appear to you symmetrical and beautiful according to my virtue, or deformed and hideous according to my vice.

Hawthorne : I see precisely your meaning, and yet I cannot realize the thought that goodness is substance.

Rivers : Never mind that for the present. As I have said, Flesh corresponds with Goodness. In the representative Church of the Jews, therefore, the priests under some circumstances, and the people under others, were commanded to eat of the flesh of the sacrifices. This was because the sacrifices represented holy things, and the flesh thereof the goodness of which they are constituted. To eat of the flesh of the sacrifices represented the appropriation of the goodnesses of heaven as the food of the soul. As you know, moreover, in the Jewish Church the people were enjoined as to what flesh they should eat and what they should avoid. They were permitted to eat of the flesh of clean animals, but not of that of unclean animals. This was because that Church was one of representatives founded on correspondences.

The eating of the flesh of clean animals represented the appropriation of spiritual purities, celestial loves, which are Good; whilst the eating of the flesh of the unclean animals would have represented the appropriation of spiritual impurities, infernal loves, which are Evil! Thus we read in Isaiah (lv. 2), " Hearken unto me, and eat ye Good, and let your soul delight itself in fatness." To eat good is evidently to receive into the spirit the substance of the Lord's flesh, as He said, " He that eateth me, even he shall live by me."

Hawthorne : I think I could show you from the Bible many passages which would not bear the test of your interpretation. Why, what is that in the Book of Revelation about eating of the flesh of kings and captains, and so on? Do you remember it?

Rivers : Very well, indeed. It is in chapter xix. verses 17 and 18. It is a vision of an angel in the sun calling the fowls to the supper of the great God, that they may eat "the flesh of kings and the flesh of captains, and the flesh of mighty men, and the flesh of horses and of them that sit on them, and the flesh of all, free and bond, both small and great."

Hawthorne : That is it. What do you make of it? I see in it merely a picture of a great battle, with the vultures gathered to a feast off the flesh of the slain.

Rivers : I am sorry for you. I don't think an angel in the sun would proclaim, as special, a thing which, alas for human evil! has been a constant occurrence in the history of the world. Moreover, I think such horrid feasts would not be called " a supper of the great God." As you have asked me, I will do my best to suggest an interpretation of this passage. The angel speaking out of the Sun is the Lord's invitation out of the fervency of his Love. The "supper of the great God" to which the birds are invited is the great Spiritual Feast, the Marriage Supper, in which the viands are composed of undying, not perishing, substances—Goodnesses and Truths in their sweetest and richest forms. The flesh of the kings, captains, and mighty men are the goodnesses of the kingly, captainly, and mighty Truths of the Word of God. *There*, in the Word of God, is the feast spread for the soul. The birds that fly in the midst of heaven, that are invited to it, are the soaring souls that have an appetite for such spiritual luxuries. Now what do you think of that?

Hawthorne: I think it remarkably clever. But you stopped in your exposition just at the point where I wanted you to go on. The flesh of the kings, captains, and mighty men may have the signification you attach to it; but what are we to say to the horses and those who sit on them—the bond and free, and so on? The horses, I imagine, are the horses of the cavalry killed in the great battle.

Rivers: It is only natural that you should think so. In the same chapter there is a description of Heaven Opened, when a white horse was seen. The opening of heaven signifies the Opening of the Word. The white horse seen when the Word is opened is the Interior Sense, then displayed pure and powerful, like a strong steed capable of bearing the soul on its heavenly journey. The flesh of the horses, therefore, is the goodness of the pure Truths of the Word in their adaptability to the wants of men. So with those that sit on them—superior truths founded on inferior truths—spiritual truths guiding

and controlling rational truths. So with the free and
bond, the small and great—truths of every kind. They
form "the supper of the great God." Their flesh is the
goodness which is their life. If we eat it we shall live.

Hawthorne: You certainly have a wonderful way of
getting out of your difficulties.

Rivers: The science of correspondences is admirably
adapted to solve all difficulties associated with the Bible.

Hawthorne: Well, but stop a minute. Did not Jesus
say, "The flesh profiteth nothing"? Does the flesh
here mean goodness? Come; does goodness profit
nothing?

Rivers: I have no doubt you think you have made a
point. But I have told you there is what the good man
calls goodness and what the evil man calls goodness.
The Christian seeks heaven and heavenly things as his
Good, and he builds up his spirit with them, and they
become, so to speak, his spiritual flesh. The worldling
seeks the World and worldly things as his Good, and in
like manner builds up his spirit with them. These latter
are Evil. The Lord says, "It is the spirit that quick-
eneth; the flesh profiteth nothing." The "spirit" there
signifies life from God, which is goodness, and the flesh
its opposite, life from self, which is evil. In the same
manner Jesus says, "That which is born of the flesh is
flesh, and that which is born of the Spirit is spirit." That
which comes from Man is Evil, and that which comes
from God is Goodness. I could give you as many passages confirmatory of this view as you could desire.
Flesh, when applied to the bad man, signifies the body
of his Evil, but when applied to the good man, the body
of his Goodness.

Hawthorne: I have been thinking as you were speaking of the passage, " Cursed is the man that maketh flesh his arm."

Rivers: Very good. That means, Cursed is the man who trusts in himself. Flesh here again corresponds with that which man has of himself, apart from God, and that is Evil. In Isaiah ix. 20 it is said that "they shall eat every man the flesh of his own arm." This refers to men who feast spiritually upon themselves—upon the evil of their own nature. So, in John i. 12, 13, the regenerate are said to be born not of the will of the flesh, but of God. The will of the flesh is the Evil of the human will. But if we continue the subject I shall have further opportunities of confirming this point. The flesh of the human body corresponds with Goodness or with Evil, according as we build either the one or the other around us by our conduct. This Goodness or Evil (which is only goodness perverted) is truly substance, and after death is as distinctly seen and felt as such as the matter of the natural body is in this world.

INTERLUDE III.

"THERE IS A SPIRITUAL BODY."

THE friends had now nearly reached their home, and they dropped their conversation, walking for a considerable time in silence, each apparently occupied with his own thoughts. At length Hawthorne, who had been somewhat impressed by the glimpses of truth which he had caught, and who had been pondering over what he had heard, spoke.

"If I understand you," he said, "we shall find ourselves in bodies with human forms after death?"

"Certainly," said Rivers; "if we exist we must have some form, and what should it be but that of man?"

"And those bodies which we shall have"—

"Don't say 'shall have,'" interrupted Rivers; "we have our spiritual bodies now: we have now the body of our *goodness* or our *evil*, and on that body even now the eye of God rests."

"Thanks," said Hawthorne; "and those bodies are according as we build around ourselves goodness or evil?"

"Yes, surely," replied Rivers.

"Then I suppose we may take it as a corollary that

we shall be fair or foul in the spiritual world according
to our conduct here?"

"You have exactly hit it," replied Rivers; "if we
build around ourselves the sweet, pure, beautiful things
of heaven—all lovely charities and fair faiths—we shall
have correspondingly sweet, pure, and lovely bodies; but
if we build around ourselves the impure and hideous
things of the infernal world, we shall have impure and
deformed bodies."

"Ah," said Hawthorne, with a sigh, "and thus every
evil thing that we do in this life has its Nemesis in the
life to come. A pleasant doctrine, surely!"

"Well," said Rivers, "we are not just now considering
what is pleasant, but what is true. The truth is, that a
corrupt soul has a body of corruption, and a pure soul a
body of purity in the world to come, where the things
that are out of order here are inevitably made right."

When Rivers and Hawthorne reached their lodgings,
they found that their friends, wearied out by their long
absence, had retired to rest. Hawthorne slept little.
The subject of the conversation was still upon his mind,
and he was the first to renew it the following morning at
the breakfast table.

CHAPTER V.

BLOOD.

Hawthorne : Well, Edith, I learned many things last night. Some of them would amaze you. You will be surprised to learn that we have not only natural but also spiritual flesh.

George : Why not?

Edith : Because it's absurd.

George : And therefore those absurd people the poets recognise it. Herbert expresses his desire to find

> " What cordials make this curious broth,
>   This broth of smells that *feeds* and *fats* my MIND."

If the mind is fed and fattened, I suppose it must have a kind of flesh.

Edith : Oh, that is only the figurative nonsense of poets.

Rivers : My dear Edith, you know that Paul says, " There is a natural body, and there is a spiritual body." Now, your natural body is a form of matter ; and your spiritual body is a form of goodness.

Edith : Goodness !

Rivers : Yes. What else should your spiritual body be made of?

Edith : Well, I don't understand it one bit ; but I suppose if we have spiritual flesh, as you call it, we have also spiritual blood.

George : Of course. What " feeds and fats the mind " makes spiritual blood.

Hawthorne : Thanks, George. My dear Rivers, really and truly I confess I am interested in your delineations of the subject. That the form of our goodness will give the appearance of bulk and symmetry to us in the spiritual world, is a novel if not a striking and acceptable idea. Moreover, I could not have believed that so many passages could be quoted from the Bible to confirm your view. But if flesh corresponds with goodness, what does blood correspond with ?

Rivers : Blood corresponds with Truth or Faith. Thus, in the passage we have already had before us, the Lord says, " Except ye eat the flesh of the Son of Man and drink His blood, ye have no life in you." While, as I have shown, the Lord's flesh signifies the Divine Goodness which we must inwardly eat, His blood signifies the Divine Truth which we must inwardly drink.

Edith : Ah, we eat and drink by faith the flesh and blood of the Lord, when we believe in His giving His body and blood on the cross for our sins.

Rivers : Not exactly so, Edith. Believing that there is bread in your pantry and wine in your cellar, is not eating and drinking of them, is it ?

Edith : Oh, certainly not ; but we cannot eat and drink the Lord's flesh and blood in that way.

Rivers : If you think of the Lord's flesh and blood as that which was seen by the Jews, which was on the cross and placed in the tomb, of course you cannot eat and drink them. But that which gives us spiritual life is the Lord's Divine Body. His Divine Body could never be touched with human hand or seen by mortal eye. His Divine Body is composed of the two things that constitute God—goodness and truth. Can you not take these into your mind or spirit as truly and really as you can take bread and wine into your body?

Mrs. Rivers: Of course. Did not the Lord say, "He that eateth *me*, even he shall live by me"? To eat the Lord is to receive Him into the spirit.

Edith: Oh, certainly, Mrs. Rivers—I see—it is, like the ravings of George's poets, figurative.

George: Here is another fit of raving, Edith—

> " I thirst for Truth,
> But shall not drink it till I reach the Source."

The source is Christ, the truth His blood. The words are Browning's.

Rivers: There is nothing figurative in the reception of the Lord in the spirit, Edith. It is fact. It is an illustration of correspondences. Flesh and blood are food for the body, and inasmuch as Divine goodness and truth are food for the soul, they correspond.

Hawthorne: That may be right so far. But now, you say our spiritual bodies are built up of goodness?

Rivers: Yes.

Hawthorne: And our spiritual veins flow with truth?

Rivers: Yes. Our affections are our spiritual veins, because they are channels for conducting truth through our mental frame.

Hawthorne: Well, our food is converted into blood.

Is our spiritual food, which you say is goodness and truth, converted into truth? That seems paradoxical.

Rivers: What we receive of God into our spirits becomes in us, first, Faith, and this feeds and nourishes our Charity. That which is goodness and truth in God becomes in man charity and faith. Faith is the blood, and charity the flesh of our spirits, and the Divine goodness and truth are constantly converted into these two essentials of the living soul.

Hawthorne: Then do you say that the Bible, being written in correspondences, is to be interpreted as signifying Truth where it mentions Blood?

Rivers: That which is blood in the literal sense is truth in the spiritual sense. The Scriptures abound with passages that are striking illustrations of this fact. It is said that we are sanctified and cleansed by the blood of Christ. But He said, "For their sakes I sanctify myself, that they also may be sanctified through the *Truth;*" and "Now ye are clean through the *Word* which I have spoken unto you." Jesus thus tells us that the *Truth,* the *Word,* is the sanctifying and cleansing force, and He does this because it is what is signified in the Scriptures by blood.

Edith: But surely, Mr. Rivers, we are sanctified and cleansed by the blood shed for us on the cross by Jesus?

Rivers: Do you think so, Edith? When and how are we sanctified and cleansed by that blood? Surely that blood was subject to the conditions of time and space. It existed only in the spot on which it was shed, and only at the moment when it gushed forth, till it was resolved into other elements. How can we be affected by it?

Edith : Are we not affected by it in faith when we believe in it?

Mrs. Rivers : I am afraid, dear, thousands believe in all the things connected with the death of Christ who are neither sanctified nor cleansed. All Christendom, where wars, murders, and robberies prevail, — where deadly antagonisms are fostered by statesmen who are the heads of churches, — teems with wickedness. If you were to ask these people to believe in the death of Christ that they might be saved, they would tell you that they did believe. The mere believing in anything done on the cross cannot make a black soul white.

Hawthorne : Of course not. That is the figment of what is called orthodoxy, and I see you are deeply touched with it, Edith. It is revolting to common sense. But still the Scriptures seem to sanction the notion. There is something about being washed in the blood, and about overcoming by the blood.

Rivers : Yes. The one is in Rev. vii. 14, and the other in Rev. xii. 11. The former speaks of those who had come "out of great tribulation, and washed their robes, and made them white in the blood of the Lamb." The blood here obviously signifies that which makes clean—the Word, which, as Jesus says, He has spoken unto us—the spiritual blood which has flowed from Him to us. The latter treats of the dragon, "that old serpent, called the Devil and Satan," and he is overcome by the Truth. In both these cases it must be perfectly clear that blood signifies truth. Nothing else can possibly be meant by the blood of the Covenant or Testament, but the truth of the Covenant or Testament.

Thus, the blood of the Covenant which Moses took and sprinkled upon the people—

Edith : But that was real blood.

Rivers : That was real natural blood, but it represented real spiritual blood, which is Truth. Moses sprinkled the people with the blood of the sacrifices, calling it the blood of the Covenant, as a correspondential act showing how Jesus, the Divine Moses, sprinkles our souls with the sanctifying power of Divine Truth.

Edith : Ah, that is altogether a new idea.

Rivers : But if new, it is not the less true. Moses sanctified Aaron and all things of the tabernacle with blood, because Truth is what sanctified Jesus, the Divine Aaron, and all things of the Church, as the Lord Himself showed when He used those words of which I have already reminded you, " For their sakes I sanctify *myself,* that *they* also may be sanctified through the Truth."

Hawthorne : I admit that to be a very striking suggestion.

Edith : But how could Jesus be signified both by Moses and Aaron ? Jesus says, " *I* sanctify *myself.*" Was He both sanctifier and sanctified ?

Rivers : Jesus was represented by both Moses and Aaron. Perhaps it may help you if I suggest that Moses represented the Lord as to His Internal or Divine nature, and Aaron the Lord as to His External or Human nature. The Divinity sanctified the Humanity by the force of its outpoured Truth. Thus Jesus sanctified Himself.

Mrs. Rivers : You must remember, Edith, that the Father and the Son are not two Divine Persons, but two Natures, the Divine and the Human in one Person.

Rivers : Aaron was sanctified by Moses through the

blood. It represents the sanctification of the Human Nature by the Divine Nature, which poured out upon it the fulness of Divine Truth. By the by, there is a passage in Zechariah (ix. 11), "As for thee also, by the blood of thy covenant I have sent forth thy prisoners out of the pit wherein is no water." The pit wherein is no water is the great deep of falsehood, in which is no spiritual refreshment. They who are imprisoned in the pit are those who are in bondage to error. The blood of the Covenant which sends forth the prisoners out of the pit is the Divine Truth of heaven which delivers men from the thraldom and darkness of falsehood. The blood of the Covenant makes the prisoners *free;* and Jesus said, "And ye shall know the *Truth*, and the Truth shall make you free."

Hawthorne: Ah, excellent! But it will hardly do. You prove too much. "Your hands are full with blood." That I think is Scripture. It refers to the wicked. Are their hands full of *truth?*

Rivers: No; of *falsehood.* The passage is in Isa. i. 15, 16: "Yea, when ye make many prayers, I will not hear: your hands are full of blood. Wash you, make you clean." To have the hands full of blood is to be defiled with falsehood. Thus again it is written by the same prophet (lix. 3), "For your hands are defiled with blood, and your fingers with iniquity." Blood here again signifies falsehood. It is precisely the same with blood as it is with flesh,—it has an opposite signification. Just as evil is the wicked man's good, so falsehood is the wicked man's truth. For this reason blood as well as flesh has an opposite signification in the Bible.

Hawthorne : That is only consistent with your former

statements, and I must confess it appears rational. Flesh and blood signify goodness and truth, or evil and falsehood?

Rivers : The reason being because the spiritual body of the regenerate is composed of goodness and truth, and that of the unregenerate of evil and falsehood. But I should like, before bringing this conversation to a close, —and I can see Edith and George are anxious to be off,—to refer to one or two passages in Ezekiel, in which blood is mentioned as the correspondence of falsehood. Thus (xvi. 6) concerning Jerusalem it is written, " When I passed by thee, and saw thee polluted in thine own blood, I said unto thee, when thou wast in thy blood, Live." Jerusalem polluted in her own blood can mean nothing else than her people defiled with their own false- hood. Indeed, in verse 9 God says, " I throughly washed away thy blood from thee." Can this refer to anything but to spiritual cleansing? God washes away errors of doctrine and life.

Hawthorne : You are having it all your own way. All I can do is to sit at your feet and learn. Tell me, there- fore, why the Jews were forbidden to eat blood. Was it because it represented truth or falsehood?

George : I should think they were forbidden to eat it because it represented falsehood.

Hawthorne : I cannot see how that can be, because it says it is the *life* of the flesh, and the flesh they ate signified goodness.

Rivers : It is a hard subject. It is one of the great deeps of the Word of God. Flesh, when not used in the sacrifices, corresponded with the affections of the natural will, which the Jews lusted to enjoy. Blood corresponds with living truth. The affections of the natural will are of the world; the living truth is of heaven. To eat flesh with the blood in the representative Church of the Jews would have denoted the reception into the spirit of the things of the world and of heaven commingled together. To eat flesh with the blood would have denoted the blending of profanities and sanctities. Hence it was forbidden. But this matter requires study.

Mrs. Rivers : In a general conversation like ours, we must be satisfied with general truths.

Rivers : Yes; but pray observe one important fact. Compare the Levitical law of *sanctification* by Blood with what Jesus says about sanctification by Truth. Compare what the prophet (Zech. ix. 11) says about the *freedom* of the prisoners by Blood, and what Jesus says about freedom by Truth. Compare what is said about *cleansing* by blood (Rev. vii. 14), and what is said about cleansing by the Word or Truth (John xv. 3). On all these points one scripture responds in the most remarkable way to the other, and confirms what I have been endeavouring to prove, that blood corresponds with truth and signifies truth in the Word of God.

INTERLUDE IV.

"FASHIONED LIKE UNTO CHRIST'S GLORIOUS BODY."

THE last utterances of Rivers seemed to be a clinching of the subject, and the little party rose from the table, and Mr. Rivers, Edith, and George quitted the room to prepare for an out-door ramble. Rivers and Hawthorne lingered behind, and the former took the opportunity to press some of the consequences of the principles he had developed.

"Now, you see," said he, "Jesus called the bread His body and the wine His blood, and said we must eat and drink of them to have life. That was because bread and wine signify the same as flesh and blood, namely, Goodness and Truth. Now observe the consequence. The body of Jesus is composed, not of material particles, but of immaterial substances. Those substances are Goodness and Truth. They constitute His glorious body. Being infinite, its beauty is ineffable. Now, we are to have in the resurrection spiritual bodies fashioned like unto Christ's glorious body, because those spiritual bodies will be composed of Goodness and Truth, the pure spiritual substance derived from Jesus by reception and absorption. Of course you know that in us goodness takes the form of Charity, and truth of Faith. Now, my dear Hawthorne, if Christ's body be insubstantial, then ours will be insubstantial. But if His body be the substance of all things that are, whether in the spiritual or natural world, then ours will be such substance too."

" It is difficult to grasp," said Hawthorne.

" Yes," said Rivers, " there is not sufficient strength in your hand at present. You can only catch hold of the perishing, shadowy things of the earth, but the enduring things of eternity are too large for the span of your four fingers and thumb."

Hawthorne looked curiously at his friend, but made no immediate reply, and the pair walked out, following the rest of the party at some distance, and presently resumed their discourse.

CHAPTER VI.

BONES.

Hawthorne: And do you say that spirits have bones?

Rivers: Certainly.

Hawthorne: But did not Jesus say, "A spirit hath *not* flesh and bones"?

Rivers: No. He said, "A spirit hath not flesh and bones as ye see *Me* have" (Luke xxiv. 39).

Hawthorne: Well, that is the same thing.

Rivers: Not quite. It cannot be interpreted to mean that spirits have not flesh and bones at all, but only that they have not *such* flesh and bones as the disciples saw the Lord to have. To those who look intently with their mental gaze, there is a vast difference between the risen Lord and the risen man. God only is real; man is comparatively unreal. Jesus is *Divine* flesh and bone, and man is at best *spiritual* flesh and bone. The difference between them is like that between substance and shadow. Thus *spiritual* flesh and bone is not such as the disciples saw the Lord have, for His was *Divine*.

Hawthorne: Well, but do you believe that the real body of Jesus rose?

Rivers: Yes. The body of Jesus was a Divine body.

It was a body of which all the universe of men and angels can eat and live for ever. It—

Hawthorne : Yes, yes ; but I mean the body of flesh and blood and bones ?

Rivers : And I mean the same. I mean the living bread which came down from heaven, and which ascended to heaven, and which to the Jews appeared in the person of Jesus clad in ordinary robes, but to the enlightened disciples with a countenance like the sun and raiment white as light. It was a matter of perception. The Jews never saw Jesus as He really was, nor did the disciples, not even on special occasions. Whatsoever might be the appearance, the Lord's body was never like that of an ordinary man. It was Divine, and therefore could not be kept in a tomb. Observe, the Lord's soul was Divine from the Father, and could not but build around itself a Divine body. Thus, as you know, a vegetable soul clothes itself with a vegetable body, an animal soul with an animal body, a human soul with a human body, and therefore a Divine soul with a Divine body. Thus what in man is natural flesh and bone, in Jesus was Divine flesh and bone. He rose *with that which in us is natural, because* IN HIM IT WAS NOT MATERIAL BUT DIVINE. In other words, He rose with that in Himself which answers to what we leave behind in the tomb. Now, perhaps, you may see something of the meaning of the phrase, " A spirit hath not flesh and bones as ye see *Me* have."

Hawthorne : Well, faintly.

Rivers : Perhaps you may see it better by and by.

Hawthorne : In the meantime, what is the correspondence of the bones ?

Rivers : We may see that from their nature and use. The bones are the *supports* of the physical structure. What supports our mental or spiritual structure? What constitutes the *framework* of our minds? The bones form the *skeleton*, which, to constitute a man, has to be clothed with flesh and blood. Cannot you see what the bones correspond with?

Hawthorne : No.

Rivers : Well, are not a man's *doctrines* of life and practice the framework of his mind, which has to be clothed with the good and true things which they teach, as the bones have to be clothed with flesh and blood?

Hawthorne : Ah, true.

Rivers : There must be something about which a man's charity and faith can cling as the flesh and blood cling around the bones. That something is his doctrine. If you can imagine a man without any doctrines, you must also imagine him without any conduct of life adhering to them. For what are doctrines? They are theories of what should be loved and done. The Mohammedan has one theory, and the Christian another. The skeleton in each case is different, but in each case it is to be clothed with living flesh. If a man had no doctrine or theory of action, he could not bring it into practice, and hence he would be like a mere lifeless nonentity.

Hawthorne : I like the thought. A man with nothing but doctrines would be spiritually a bony skeleton, and if he wished to be a living man, with warm flesh and blood, he would have to bring those doctrines into practice.

Rivers : Precisely. Now that is why so many strange things are written about the bones in the Scriptures.

Hawthorne: Ah, you mean about *talking* bones, *rejoicing* bones, *flourishing* bones, *disjointed* bones, and so forth?

Rivers: I don't exactly follow you. I remember, however, that the Psalmist cries, "All my bones shall *say*, Lord, who is like unto thee?" Bones that so express themselves are doctrines whose utterances are actions. The Psalmist, too, says, "I tell all my bones," by which he means that his doctrines are despised and mocked at. So when he says, "All my bones are out of joint," he obviously refers to spiritual troubles and dislocations.

Hawthorne: Well, is that what is meant by the rib?

Rivers: Something like it. The rib was made into a woman. A doctrine is made alive and human when it is built up and surrounded with all the sweetnesses and graces of feminine humanity by the Divine fashioning hand. There is a bit of hardness somewhere in us that needs to be removed, like the rib from Adam's side, and the soft flesh closed up instead. The doctrine that is our rib-bone is the theory of unregenerate man that Self must be served and sought. That needs removal and raising up into a sweeter and nobler Self, filled with the life of God, and adorned with the beauty of heaven, and which we may cleave to and make one with ourselves.

Hawthorne: Oh! that is the way you smooth over all difficulties, is it? I suppose the vision of the valley full of dry bones is as simple to you as the multiplication table?

Rivers: No, no. Something, however, may be known of it. The valley full of dry bones is the mind full of dry doctrines. The souls of thousands at the present day are only valleys of dry bones. The breath of the

Lord that stirred the bones is the Divine influence that enters the mind and gives some stirrings of life to the dead theories scattered there. The coming together of the bones is the arrangement of these dead doctrines by living influences; and the flesh, and sinews, and skin that came upon them signify the goodnesses of various kinds that gather symmetrically round them.

Hawthorne : But, if I remember rightly, after the sinews and flesh came upon the bones, they were still dead. How was that? If the sinews and flesh mean goodnesses of various kinds, it seems strange that they should not have given life. According to your views, to be good is to be alive.

Rivers : Not necessarily. There are two sorts of goodnesses. When we think we work from ourselves, our works are dead. It is only when we acknowledge that we have nothing good about us, save that which we receive from the Lord, that our works are alive. Hence a further heavenly influence or breath was needful to cause the "exceeding great army" to live.

Hawthorne : But, after all, the prophet applies the vision to the restoration of Israel to their own land.

Rivers : That is the literal sense of the vision. I have given you the spiritual sense.

Hawthorne : Is there not another parable of Ezekiel's about boiling and burning bones?

Rivers : Yes. It is in the 24th chapter. The Israelites were told to set on a pot and to put into it flesh and bones, to "fill it with the choice bones," and to "take the choice of the flock, and burn also the bones under it, and make it boil well, and let them seethe the bones of it therein." This was a picture of the "bloody city." It was a parable of their own states and doings. They were thus to offer violence to the natural flesh and bones as a parable exhibiting their own spiritual correspondence. They had violated every principle of goodness and truth. The choice things of heaven, including every doctrine taught them, they had polluted. Hence also the parable was a picture of their own condemnation. You may learn from this why it was forbidden to the Jews to break a bone of the paschal lamb (Num. ix. 12), and why the Psalmist (xxxiv. 20) says of the righteous, " He keepeth all his bones ; not one of them is broken," which John (xix. 36) applies to the Lord : " For these things were done that the scripture should be fulfilled, A bone of Him shall not be broken." The paschal lamb represented the pure goodness of innocence, and its bones the doctrine which supports it. This doctrine is to be preserved inviolable. Can you imagine that God would have prescribed such observances without some such signification ? The Lord keeping the bones of the good man signifies the preservation within him of those truths by which he is kept upright. That a bone of the Lord was not broken, signifies that every heavenly doctrine is preserved whole.

Hawthorne : But surely you will not maintain that this principle can be applied to all parts of what you call the Word of God with similar results ?

Rivers : I do. You must, however, remember that there are the doctrines of the good, and also the doctrines of the evil. The former are truths, the latter falsehoods. Bones, therefore, may signify doctrinal truths or doctrinal errors. There are examples of both in the Scriptures.

Hawthorne : Is that how you interpret the law about a person being unclean if he touched the bone—dead, I suppose—of a man?

Rivers : Certainly. But, of course, you remember that the bones of Elisha revived a dead man, and caused him to stand upon his feet (2 Kings xiii. 21). That was in consequence of the representative character of Elisha. He represented the Lord, and his bones, of course, the Divine doctrinal truths. These confer spiritual life. But it was ordained that an Israelite should be unclean if he touched a dead body, or a bone of a man, or a grave, because these things correspond with the dead things of the Selfhood, the bone with the dead doctrines of the man of sin. For the same reason Jehovah threatens (Jer. viii. 1, 2) that the bones of the false kings, princes, priests, prophets, and inhabitants of Jerusalem shall be brought out of their graves and spread forth to the sun, moon, and stars which they had worshipped, and should not be buried, but become offal on the face of the earth. You will see the significancy of this. The bones of these false children of the Church are the doctrinals of the world and of self, to which they lived, and which are threatened with dishonour and dispersion. So the Pharisees were called by our Lord "whited sepulchres" full of dead men's bones and all uncleanness. The Pharisaic soul is a depository of dead falsehoods and other spiritual uncleannesses.

Hawthorne: You have succeeded beyond my expectations. Flesh, Blood, and Bone,—these form the body of a man.

Rivers : Yes. The material body as to its most general constituents.

Hawthorne: And Charity, Faith, and Doctrine form the body of a man's spirit?

Rivers: Yes. The substance and the framework of his mind. By the by, do you remember that Joseph adjured the children of Israel to carry up with them his bones from Egypt to Canaan?

Hawthorne: I had forgotten that.

Rivers: Well, the progress of the Israelites from Egypt to Canaan was representative of the progress of the Church and of the human soul from the bondage of nature to the freedom of spiritual life. In this progress it is essential that the doctrines of the Divine Joseph should be carried forward and accompany us in all the way. But flesh, blood, and bones do not form the whole body.

Hawthorne: Indeed? What else is there?

Rivers: Why, the skin,—the covering to it all; and the hair a covering to the skin. So, Hawthorne, you see, we have two other subjects to consider before we have done with the correspondence of the general features of the body.

E

CHAPTER VII.

THE SKIN.

Edith : Here are Mr. Rivers and father, and arguing again. Let us join them.

Hawthorne (to Rivers) : The Skin ? What can be the correspondence of the Skin ?

Rivers : Cannot you perceive ? It corresponds with that portion of a man's spirit which you can *see.*

Edith : See ? You cannot see any portion of a man's spirit.

Rivers : Cannot you see a man's spirit in his works ? You cannot see a man's flesh, blood, or bones, but you can see his Skin. In just the same manner you cannot see a man's charity, faith, or doctrines, but you can see his Deeds. Now we have skins of all sorts. There is the black skin, the olive skin, the red skin, and the white skin, and by the various kinds of skins we know the various races or tribes of men upon the earth. The external appearance indicates the internal character. In the same way there are men whose *deeds* are of every shade from pure white to deep black, and these deeds — this spiritual skin — reveal their internal spiritual nature.

Hawthorne: I think the skin is spoken of in the vision of Ezekiel to which you lately referred.

Rivers: The flesh came up upon the bones, and "the skin covered them above." The flesh, as we have said, corresponds with that charity or goodness which constitutes our spiritual bodies, and the skin which came up upon the flesh corresponds with the loving life in which charitable affections terminate.

Hawthorne: Ah, the skin is the external covering or termination of the flesh ; it is a preservative of the more delicate tissues beneath ; it is the sensitive organ of touch. How in these respects do you trace your correspondence ?

Rivers: I have already referred to the well-known fact that good affections must necessarily *terminate* in or *cover themselves* with a life woven of good deeds. Now a good life operates to *preserve* the good affections from which it proceeds, for anything that does not go forth to an end perishes. What would become of our charity if it never came forth in loving act ? Then, again, it is by means of active operation that we *touch*, as it were, the minds of our fellow-men, and find them smooth and agreeable or harsh and unpleasant.

Hawthorne: You remind me of a beautiful bit by Ruskin. He says, "Those who hold that man can be saved by thinking rightly, by word instead of act, by wish instead of work—these are the true fog children ; clouds these without water ; bodies these of putrescent vapour and skin without blood or flesh."

Rivers: Ah, very good. The skin without blood or flesh is a life without charity or faith beneath it.

George: The leprosy was a disease in the skin. I

suppose all the laws about it in Leviticus were on the ground of its correspondence.

Rivers : Undoubtedly. The leprosy was a disease having its origin in the blood and exhibiting itself in the skin, whereon came certain plague spots. It corresponds with that spiritual disease in man's interior nature which expresses itself in his exterior life. Every evil deed arising from an impure faith corrupting the soul as impure blood corrupts the body is a leprous scab on our spiritual skin. That is why the leper was cast out of the camp of the Israelites, and had to go forth crying " Unclean, unclean."

Edith : Mr. Rivers ! I should think the reason was because the leprosy was a contagious disease. I don't see why we should look for strange and hidden meanings in the Bible when there is a very plain and simple one.

George : Was that the reason why clothes that had the leprosy were said to be unclean and had to be burnt, and houses that had the leprosy should be condemned as unclean and have the affected stones taken out of them and cast into an unclean place ?

Edith : Don't make me despise you, George ! Who ever heard of clothes and houses having the leprosy ?

Rivers : That shows how little the book of Leviticus is studied even by such good Christians as you, Edith. In the 13th and 14th chapters you will find that garments (xiii. 47, 59) really had what was called a leprosy, which had to be dealt with by the priest, and that houses (xiv. 34, 48) were affected with the same disease. If there was no other way of getting rid of it, the house had to be broken down and destroyed.

Edith : Ah, that was in the same way as clothes and

houses in these days, in cases of fevers and smallpox, are disinfected.

Rivers : Oh, dear me, no ! The clothes and houses really had the leprosy, and the spots spread on the garments and the walls. Read those chapters and you will know all about it. This arose from correspondence. The garment, the outer covering of the body, has a similar correspondence to the skin. The plague spot on the garment denoted the plague spot in the Christian's life. The house corresponds with man, whose soul is a house of God and whose body is the house of the soul. The walls of the house signify the same as the skin of the body, and the plague spot in the walls corresponds with the evil deed that makes the external life unclean. The ultimate breaking down of the house, if the leprosy in it could not be stayed, represented the utter breakdown and destruction of the soul if the conduct cannot be purified.

Hawthorne : That is the most remarkable illustration we have yet had. I certainly had missed the fact that clothes and houses were said to have the leprosy.

Rivers : The Scriptures abound with remarkable illustrations respecting the leprosy. But let me for a moment more speak of the correspondence of the skin, the garment, and the house. The garment is, so to speak, an outer skin, and a house is an outer garment. Now the hair is, in relation to the garment, the cap or hat ; and in relation to the house, the roof. The skin is, in relation to the garment, the coat or cloak ; and in relation to the house, the walls. Now all these—the skin, the garments, and the house—have reference to the outer things of conduct by which we are spiritually clothed and surrounded, and the leprosy in them to the evils that mar our conduct and defile it with spots.

George : I suppose the cleansing of the leper denoted the cleansing of the leprous soul.

Rivers : Yes. Naaman the Assyrian was miraculously cured of leprosy by bathing in Jordan seven times at the command of Elisha (2 Kings v. 14). Our lives are purified from evil deeds by complete spiritual washing in the living waters in obedience to the Lord, who says, " Wash you, make you clean ; put away the evil of your doings from before mine eyes." Again, Jesus cleansed the leper with His touch. The skin of the Lord of sweetness and health came in contact with that of the Man of foulness and disease. The skin of the Lord corresponds with the ultimate forms through which the Divine virtue issues, and the skin of the leper with the ultimate forms in which human vice terminates. The Divine goodness is the antidote to human evil. The sweetness and health of the Lord banishes the foulness and disease of the man. Moreover, the outermost of the Lord's body corresponds with the outermost of the Word, that is, the sense of the letter. When this sense really *touches* the leprous soul it is clean.

Mrs. Rivers : When Moses came down from the Mount, after he had been talking with Jehovah, it is written that the skin of his face so shone that the children of Israel could not come nigh to him, and he had to put a veil upon his face.

Rivers : The skin of Moses shining signifies the ineffable glory of the Divine love and wisdom manifested in the Divine providence, which no man can look upon with undazed eye.

Edith : You are changing your doctrine, Mr. Rivers. You said the skin corresponds with outward deeds. Now you say it signifies Divine Providence.

Rivers : Certainly, Edith. What is the Divine Providence but the Divine operation?

Edith : But Moses is not God. What has the Divine Providence to do with Moses' skin and its shining?

Rivers : I have before explained that Moses represented the Lord. The skin of Moses therefore corresponds with the external things, the emanations from the Lord in the last degree, and these are the glorious acts of Creation, Redemption, and Providence. Moses also represented the Word, and his shining skin the letter or outer covering of the Word bright with the light glowing from within.

George : Edith's orthodoxy is alarmed at the suggestion that the Bible means so much !

Edith : I always thought the Bible was so plain that any one could understand it. But according to you, Mr. Rivers, it requires the study of a lifetime only to know a little bit of it.

Rivers : So it does, my dear. It treats of things you cannot see and of which without it you must remain in ignorance. It treats of heaven and hell and the deep mysteries of the spirit within you. You cannot expect to learn about unseen things without study.

Hawthorne : No, Edith. The short and easy method of accepting the Scriptures that prevails among your friends is, I am afraid, responsible for most of the scepticism amongst us. I know it is responsible for much of mine.

Rivers : There is one other passage respecting the skin

to which I should like to refer. In Lamentations (iv. 8) it is written, "Their visage is blacker than a coal; they are not known in the streets; their skin cleaveth to their bones; it is withered, it is become like a stick." There is the black visage, the black skin. It corresponds with the darkened life, for it describes the Church in its degradation and misery. The withered skin that cleaves to the bone is the withered life beneath which there is no charity and no faith, only bare doctrine.

Hawthorne : Very suggestive. I am afraid that is the character of thousands of Christians. Their religion has no flesh and blood—no goodness and truth, no charity and faith. It is a thing of Bone and withered Skin— Doctrine merely, and a withered Life.

CHAPTER VIII.

THE HAIR.

Hawthorne: I think you spoke of the correspondence of the hair. During this half-hour's silence, I have been trying to think what it can be. Bones, Flesh, Blood, Skin! Doctrines covered with Charity, Faith, and a beautiful smooth Life! I can see that; but I cannot get beyond it.

Rivers: You must think of the position, nature, and use of the hair.

Hawthorne: Well, as to its position, it is exterior to the skin,—the most external thing of the body.

Rivers: Of course. Therefore it must represent the most external things of the soul. What are they? Internal things are those of charity and faith, which are connected with heaven and the eternities.

Hawthorne: Ah! then I suppose the hair corresponds with the external things connected with Nature and its temporalities.

Rivers: The outermost is also lowermost. The hair, therefore, corresponds with the lowest things associated with our spirits. The lowest things are those of sense and the world. They are the things in which the life of the soul terminates, as the life of the body terminates in the hair.

Hawthorne: Then why was so much account made of the hair in the Jewish Church, and why were they forbidden to make themselves bald? I should have thought that it would be well to get rid of the outermost or lowermost things of sense and the world, eh?

Rivers: Certainly not. Suppose the outermost things of the house—the tiles or slates on the roof, or the cement and paint on the walls—go, what then? What would become of the things inside? Would not they begin to go too? Suppose the outermost fibre of your garments is brushed away, would not the essential fibre within fall to pieces?

Hawthorne: Ah, I never thought of that!

Rivers: Now, the hair represents the same as the outermost gloss of the garment and the outermost material of the house. The spiritual things of the soul would perish if they were not preserved by its natural things, which are those connected with our sensations.

Hawthorne: There is not much "preservation" connected with the hair, is there?

Rivers: Certainly. The hair preserves the head from scorching heats and chill blasts. So the highest things of the soul, denoted by the head, as we shall see, are preserved by the lowest things, denoted by the hair. The hair thus signifies the lowest and outermost things of the natural mind, which constitute the ultimate covering of the spiritual mind. The Lord says, "The very hairs of your head are all numbered." Of course you will easily believe that this does not mean that our natural hairs are all known. That would be useless and absurd.

It means that the very lowest and outermost things of our life, those connected with the world and all its sensations, are seen of our Heavenly Father; and they are so seen because He perceives the causes—the internal sources—from which they spring. When it is said, "The very hairs of your head are numbered," it means that we are known of God thoroughly and completely down to the lowest and minutest things of our everyday life.

Hawthorne: Then the Israelites were not to make themselves bald because of the signification of baldness?

Rivers: That is so. To be bald denoted the absence of natural truth, such as that of the letter of the Word. A man who has no historical or scientific truths—no truths respecting social and neighbourly life—is like a bald man. The priests and people were forbidden to shave off the hair of their heads, or to cut the corner of their beards for the dead. The reason was because of the correspondence of the hair. We must not deprive ourselves of ultimate truths, but under all circumstances preserve them, because in their possession is power. You remember the children who called Elisha, baldhead. Two she-bears came out of the wood and tare forty-and-two of them. Now Elisha represented the Word of God, which he spoke. Calling Elisha baldhead is declaring there is no ultimate or literal truth in the Word. When people read the Scriptures and throw it contemptuously on one side, declaring that its science is folly, its history falsehood, its miracles absurdities, and its precepts of life impossible, they are calling Elisha baldhead,—they are declaring that no natural or literal truth adorns the Divine messenger from God to men! What are the consequences? They regard as a lie what is given to restrain the wild beasts within, and, all restraint being removed, those beasts leap out of the deep wood-like recesses of their evil nature and rend and destroy man's spiritual life.

Hawthorne: Good. But why forty-and-two of them?

Rivers: Because of the representative character of that number. Forty-and-two signifies blasphemy.

Hawthorne: Blasphemy!

Rivers: Yes. Don't you remember what is written in Rev. xiii. 5 concerning the beast with seven heads and ten horns, which had power to blaspheme forty-and-two months?

Hawthorne: I had forgotten it. It is certainly remarkable.

George: Of course the great strength of Samson, which lay in his hair, had something to do with the correspondence.

Edith: Oh, that was God's will! If God had willed that Samson should be strong with a bald head, and weak with a hairy head, He could have done so.

George: Yes. Thou thinkest He is altogether such an one as thyself! Caliban in his island reasoned thus: "As it likes me each time, I do. So He." He thought that God is guided by human caprices. But God always wills in one way—in the way of order and right. It is impossible that the Divine Will should be erratic and uncertain in its operation, as you seem to think, Edith.

Edith: We are told in the Bible that *all* things are possible with God.

George: All *right* things are, Edith; not any one *wrong* thing.

Rivers: Because of the correspondence of the hair,

the law of the Nazariteship was established in the Jewish Church. In Numbers vi. 5, it is said that no razor shall come upon the Nazarite's head, and till he separated himself to the Lord, he was to be holy and let the locks of the hair of his head grow. The Nazarite, you see, signifies the holy man, and he is the holy man who dedicates to God the *outermost extremes of his life*,—the most remote and trivial things of nature,—whose every act is sanctified, even to the simple concerns of domestic relationships and business affairs.

Hawthorne : Ah, such a man is strong !

Rivers : Samson's strength lay in his hair, for reasons which may be variously suggested. First, he represented the Lord, the Infinitely Strong, and whose strength is in the last things of the natural universe, where it terminates. Secondly, he represented the Word, the Divinely Strong, whose strength is in the least things, the letters and syllables, with which God's goodness and truth are clothed, and which find entrance into human minds to influence them. Lastly, he represented the Good Man, who is strong because the Divine Life begins in his soul's heart, and flows out into his soul's hairs, thus affecting him from first to last.

Edith : Mr. Rivers ! " Soul's heart" and " soul's hairs !" How very absurd !

Rivers : Not at all, Edith. The heart of the soul is the Will, the seat of our affections and emotions, as you will learn by and by, if you be attentive. And the hairs of the soul are, as you might have learned already, its outermost truths in action.

Hawthorne : Samson was weak when his hair was shorn. Is that a historical truth, or only an allegory ?

Rivers : A historical truth. Before Christ's coming correspondences had power, and those who were skilled in them could work magic, as did the Egyptians. Samson was a Nazarite, and his natural strength was associated with his hair, because God's strength, the Word's strength, the Good Man's strength, is associated with ultimate truths, with which the hair corresponds. The lowest thing of a house is its foundation, that is where its strength lies. The letter of the Word is its foundation, the higher senses stand upon it. In the letter, therefore, is the strength of the Word. Thus it is written, "If the foundations are destroyed, what shall the righteous do?" If it were not for the letter of the Word, God would have no power over men. Samson had such great natural strength, as a condition of his letting the seven locks of the hair of his head grow, because he represented the Lord, the Word, the Good Man, with their interior goodness flowing out and down to the remotest things of life, and in that flowing down is manifested strength.

Hawthorne : It is the only rational explanation of Samson's strength and his hair that I have ever heard attempted.

Edith : That is how you became a sceptic, pa',—by wanting rational explanations of things before you would believe them.

Hawthorne : Well, Edith, they who believe without understanding don't half believe. They have only a blind persuasion.

Rivers : Have you ever noticed the fifth chapter of Ezekiel and the enacted parable of the hair which it contains? The prophet is commanded to shave off the hair

of his head and beard, and to divide it into three parts.
He was then to burn a third part with fire, to smite a
third part about with a knife, and to scatter a third part
in the wind. This was a correspondential act. It
represented what the Israelites had themselves done.
By violating all that low order of truths committed to
them, they had, as it were, shorn the Lord, the Word,
themselves, of all spiritual hair. They had destroyed
those truths by the fire of their lusts, had smitten them
by the knife of falsehood, and had scattered them by the
winds of erroneous doctrine.

Edith : Why, Mr. Rivers, this was a sign of what was
to happen to the Israelites. What was done to the hair
was to be done to them, as is said in the chapter.

Rivers : True, Edith. He who destroys the truths
given for his guidance and salvation, destroys himself.
Do you remember the passage (Jer. vii. 28, 29), " *Truth*
is perished and is cut off from their mouth : cut off thine
hair, O Jerusalem, and cast it away." How could that be
unless the hair is the correspondence of truth in its ultimate form ? *Truth* is cut off ; therefore cut off thine *hair !*

Hawthorne : What do you think of that, Edith ? Even
you must acknowledge there is something in that.

Rivers : You will all remember the wonderful prophecy
in Isaiah (vii. 20), in which it is said that the Lord will
shave with a hired razor, "by the king of Assyria, the
head, and the hair of the feet, and also consume the
beard "? The king of Assyria deprives Israel of its
spiritual hair, when the keen reasoning of self-authorized
philosophy deprives the Word and the Church of all
literal truth. This prophecy is wondrously fulfilled
at this day. The kings of Assyria are the Huxleys and

Darwins. They shave away every vestige of truth from the external of the Word. Its cosmogony is a fiction : its history is fable; its prophecy ranting poetry; its precepts foolish and impracticable. Every external truth from the crown of the head to the sole of the foot is swept away from the sacred Scriptures. That occurs when there is no faith in the Church, when the Church is bald of truth ; and I am afraid we are not far off that state at the present moment.

INTERLUDE V.

"THE GLORY OF THE CELESTIAL IS ONE, AND THE
GLORY OF THE TERRESTRIAL IS ANOTHER."

THAT same evening our little party were sitting at the
head of the pier enjoying the quiet hour of sunset. The
soft fresh breeze, the crimson lights flung over the vast of
waters, and the music of the waves lashing the piles
beneath, had for them a peculiar fascination, and they
were all silently drinking in the rich influence of the
moment. Suddenly their attention was attracted by a
crowd and commotion at some distance up the beach,
and Rivers, Hawthorne, and George, hurrying to learn
the cause, found that the body of a sailor had been
washed ashore. There it lay in all its dead helplessness,
the hair still washed to and fro by the waters rippling on
the sands, the limbs listless, and the eyes staring.

The poor fellow in the effort to save himself had
evidently drawn off one of his boots, but otherwise the
body was clothed. The sight produced a shock on the
minds of our friends, unused to such spectacles, and they
looked on in awed silence till the body was borne away
to the dead-house.

"What will they do with him now?" said Hawthorne;
"bury him?"

"Him! What *him?*" said Rivers. "Do you suppose any one can bury a man? *He* and that carcase are two different things. You cannot inter a soul."

"Ah, yes, of course; the man is a soul now, a disembodied soul, and that, after all your talk, I can only think of as a vapour or shadow. I have heard, and, as I have thought, understood, all that you have said about the substance of charity, faith, and doctrine being the substance of the spiritual body, but it all escapes me. I cannot retain it for an hour at a time."

"Materialistic ideas cannot tolerate the entrance of spiritual thought. Now let us be seriously contemplative, my dear Hawthorne. Cease to attach importance to these worthless grains of sand on which we are treading, and lift your mind to the consideration of the thought that there may be a heaven and that it must have a foundation for the feet of the angels, that foundation being the Divine truths on which they stand. Surely Divine truths are more solid than sand?"

"I see that idea," said Hawthorne.

"Well, then, to recur to our subject. Is the body of our Love less real than the body of our flesh? Is the Faith that enriches and feeds our Love less real than the blood that feeds the natural body? Are the Doctrines that build up our mental frame less sound and strong than the bones that build up our physical frame? Is the good man's Life less white and smooth than his skin? Are the Knowledges which overcurl his intellect less graceful than the hair that adorns his head? But you will say they are only ideal, not real"——

"Excuse me," said George; "Mrs. Browning, in *Aurora Leigh,* says,

> "' Better call THE REAL,
> And certain to be called so presently,
> When things shall have their names.'

Ideal here ; real there !"

"Ideal to the natural mind," said Rivers ; "real to the spiritual mind. The spiritual eye rests upon the body of the good man's Love, and sees it to be fair. The more perfect therefore the love of the angel, the more beautiful his body. So with the blood. If a spirit has a weak Faith, his Blood pulsates feebly. If a spirit has unsound Doctrines, there is no soundness in his Bones. If the Life be fair, so is the Skin. Thus an African being good has a white skin in the spiritual world, and an Englishman being evil a black one. So some have flowing locks and others bald heads. Those who are bald of knowledges appear personally bald, and are not merely so in an ideal sense."

"And you really believe all this ?" asked Hawthorne in astonishment.

"I were else blind and deaf to God, the most persistent and perceivable form and the most distinct voice in Nature."

"My dear Mr. Hawthorne," said George, "you should study the despised poets. Listen to this :

> "' Not a natural flower can grow on earth
> Without a flower upon the spiritual side,
> Substantial, archetypal, all aglow
> With blossoming causes, not so far away
> That we, whose spirit sense is somewhat cleared,
> May not catch something of the bloom and breath.'

If there are flowers on the spiritual side to enable natural flowers to grow, don't you think it necessary that there should be men on the spiritual side to enable natural men to grow?"

"Tush, boy!" said Hawthorne, "poets can imagine anything. I believe we owe our religion to the poets."

"I would rather owe it," said Rivers, "to the poets than the scientists, who propound one theory to-day and another to-morrow. If religion were founded on science, we should have to change it with every new edition of the Encyclopædia Britannica. We should have a gospel according to Ptolemy, superseded by an Epistle of Copernicus, and amplified and enlarged by an Apocalypse by Darwin and Huxley, the whole to be thrown down and a new one built up in the year 2000 by one of their descendants, in consequence of the invention of more powerful and refined instruments of observation."

"Well," said Hawthorne, "I like your enthusiasm, and wish it were contagious."

"If you are not tired of our topics, we will continue them," said Rivers.

"Tired!" said Hawthorne; "they abound with interest, though I must confess myself a dull scholar."

"Then we will proceed to some of the organs of the Senses," said Rivers.

"With all my heart," said Hawthorne.

The friends were here joined by Mrs. Rivers and Edith, and the discussion was dropped, as they were very soon relating the circumstance of the incident on the beach. Nothing more was said till the next morning, when the ladies were making preparations for a country drive, and the gentlemen found themselves for half an hour alone.

CHAPTER IX.

THE EYE.

Hawthorne: You said you would take up the subject of the correspondence of the organs of sense and speech.

Rivers: Certainly. Let us take first the Eye, the organ of sight.

Hawthorne: What do you say is its correspondence?

Rivers: I would rather you should answer. The use of the eye is to see natural things. It, therefore, corresponds with that power by which we see spiritual things. What do we see spiritual things with?

Hawthorne: Well, I suppose you refer to the Mind?

Rivers: We see laws, facts, principles, by means of the Intellect or Understanding. The Intellect, therefore, is our spiritual eye. If you *see* there is a God and a heaven, you will see it by the exercise of the *Understanding.*

Hawthorne: Ah, very good. I expected something of the sort.

Rivers: The Eye corresponds with the Understanding, first, because of its receptive power; and next, because of its perceptive power. The eye is receptive of natural light; the understanding of spiritual light, that is, truth. There is the darkened eye and the darkened intellect. Into the one falls no sunbeam, into the other no God-beam.

George : This, I suppose, is what blind Milton sang of—

" So much the rather thou, celestial light,
  Shine inward, and the mind, through all her powers,
  Irradiate ; there plant eyes, all mist from thence
  Purge and disperse, that I may see and tell
  Of things invisible to mortal sight."

"Celestial light," I imagine, is heavenly light, and heavenly light is truth.

Rivers : Yes. The intellect is receptive of heavenly light from God as the eye is receptive of natural light from the sun ; hence the one corresponds to the other.

Hawthorne : Very good. That is a point I cannot contest.

Rivers : That is what is meant in the words of the Psalmist : "Lighten mine eyes lest I sleep the sleep of death " (Ps. xiii. 3). You cannot imagine that the Psalmist asked for natural light to keep him from death. He prayed for spiritual light.

Hawthorne : Of course. I clearly see that, the Psalms being poems, this was a poetical expression.

Rivers : It was an expression grounded in corre-spondences. The understanding is the spiritual organ adapted to the reception of truth which is spiritual light, and the eye a natural organ adapted to the reception of that effluence of the sun which we call natural light. You see the perfection of the corre-spondence ?

Hawthorne: I see the analogy.

Rivers: Something more than an analogy. The natural eye is the organ which the intellect necessitates. The understanding could be nothing without the eye, nor the eye without the understanding. Thus spiritual sight causes natural sight, and the spiritual eye and the natural eye are to each other as cause and effect. The law is everywhere observed in the Scriptures. Thus we read of the open eye and of the blind eye. The open eye is, of course, the enlightened understanding, and the blind eye the obscured understanding.

Hawthorne: Ah, the open eye being in fact the receptive and the blind eye the non-receptive mind.

Rivers: Put it so. Again, we read of those who "have eyes to see and see not" (Ezek. xii. 2). The people referred to are those who have the power to perceive truth and do not exercise it. I might quote scores of passages to the same purpose. The eye of God signifies the Divine intelligence and foresight, and thence Providence; while the eye of man signifies human intelligence and the intellect which exercises it. Thus the four animals full of eyes before and behind, round about God's throne, as described in the Apocalypse (iv. 6-11), and which never rest day nor night, crying, "Holy, holy, holy, Lord God Almighty, which was and is and is to come," are descriptive of the Divine Providence. They are four, looking to *all* points of spirit and nature. They are full of eyes—all sight, all intelligence. The eyes are before and behind—signifying the intelligence that in the present comprehends the past and the future—all states and times behind and all states and times before.

Hawthorne: A grand and sublime thought.

Rivers: And true! So the Lamb in the midst of the throne is said to have seven eyes. The Lamb is Jesus. His seven eyes signify Omniscience, that is, of course, all intelligence, all sight! In the first chapter of the Apocalypse the Lord's eyes are said to be as a flame of fire, to denote the presence of the fire of love in the Divine Wisdom.

Hawthorne: Yes, I see the reason for your assertion of the correspondence, and I see the aptness of your illustrations. But I imagine there are some passages in the Scriptures that will not so readily answer your purpose. For instance, "If thy right eye offend thee, pluck it out and cast it from thee" (Matt. v. 29). It would hardly do to pluck out the whole understanding, would it? And how could it be done?

Rivers: Do you suppose that there is any offence in the natural organ? Offences must be in the mind, surely. If the mouth blasphemes, or the eye looks unchastely, the evil must certainly be in the man himself, and not in the mere medium. Now it is said here, "If thy right eye offend thee." The eye is the intelligence, —the right eye the intelligence from goodness, and the left eye the intelligence from truth. You will therefore see that the *offending* right eye must be the intelligence from evil, — that is to be plucked out of the spiritual system.

Hawthorne: What, do you even go so far as to make distinctive differences between the right and left side of the body?

Rivers: Certainly. There is a separate cause for every separate effect. But more of that by and by. Your suggestion about the offending right eye reminds

me of the words of Jesus, as in Matt. vi. 22 : " The light
of the body is the eye : if therefore thine eye be single,
thy whole body shall be full of light.   But if thine eye be
evil, thy whole body shall be full of darkness."   Can you
understand that in relation to the natural organ?   To
understand it you must think of the spiritual body
and the spiritual eye.   The understanding is the eye of
the spirit.   If the understanding be simple, the spirit is
full of the light of truth ; but if the understanding be evil,
the spirit is full of the darkness of falsehood.   Can you
understand the passage without that gloss?

Hawthorne : No.   You must be right in that matter.

Rivers : What is the beam and the mote in the eye?
Is not the mote in the brother's eye a small intellectual
defect, and the beam in our own eye a large intellectual
defect?

Hawthorne : I cannot deny it ; but yet I cannot
accept your wide-reaching conclusions about correspondence, causes and effects, and so forth.   Is intelligence the cause of sight, and ignorance the cause of
blindness?

Rivers : I may answer your question so far as to say
that if there were among mankind perfect wisdom there
would be perfect sight, and if there were no folly there
would be no blindness.   I don't say that wise men have
all perfect eyes, and fools alone are blind.   There is
disorder in the world, and correspondences do not
operate perfectly as they would in an orderly world.
That Jesus considered natural blindness had something
to do with spiritual blindness, is clear from the fact that
when He opened the blind man's eyes He spoke of Himself as the " light of the world " (John ix. 5), and added

(39), "For judgment am I come into this world, that they which see not might see, and that they which see might be made blind," while He also referred to the Pharisees as not blind, and therefore having sin. You can only understand all this as having relation to spiritual things. He is the spiritual light of the world. He came to enlighten those willing to understand, to darken those unwilling. Again, not being blind to truth and duty, we have sin if we do it not.

Hawthorne : That is all very obvious. Those observations about spiritual things were called forth by the miracle said to have been wrought, but it does not follow that there was the intimate relation suggested by your idea of correspondence.

Rivers : Well, how did the Lord cure the blind man? He spat on the ground, made clay of the spittle, anointed his eyes, and sent him to wash in the pool of Siloam. That describes correspondentially how our understandings are opened to heavenly things. The Lord spitting upon the ground signifies the Divine influence touching the good ground of the heart, and affecting it and bringing the new state thus formed to operate upon the intellect, which is cleansed by the waters of the Word.

Hawthorne : What is that?

Rivers : Why, think you, did the Lord observe such a strange process in giving this blind man his sight? No one can understand apart from the law of correspondences. First, the Lord is the Infinite God. Next, His spittle is the Divine Truth proceeding from Him. The Ground is the ground of that Affection in man which receives the truth. The Clay formed of the spittle and the ground is the New State of Affection wrought in us by the Divine Operation. The anointing the man's eyes with the clay is expressive of the act of bringing the new and good Affection to bear upon the Intellect. So far all is of God. The work performed is of an interior character, touching the heart and thence the intellect. The rest is of the man himself. He must cleanse himself of exterior evils by washing in the waters of the Word. Then his understanding is clear, and he sees in perfect light what was before obscure and what is hidden from others.

Hawthorne: And you really trace all that in these circumstances?

Rivers: Undoubtedly. It is something like what is written in Rev. iii. 17, 18, where the Lord says, " Because thou knowest not that thou art blind, I counsel thee to anoint thine eyes with eye-salve, that thou mayest see." Of course, you perceive that this blindness is spiritual? What is the eye-salve that is a cure for spiritual blindness? That also must be spiritual. It is goodness—a state of goodness brought about by the spittle of Divine Truth commingled with the ground of our affection.

Hawthorne: Well, all this surpasses my comprehension. It is incredible. You make every little circumstance, as well as every little act and object, a correspondence.

Rivers: Of course. Every little circumstance, act, and object in the natural world must have a cause in the spiritual world—the world of mind—and correspond therewith.

George: You are one of those persons, Mr. Hawthorne, of whom Emerson speaks. He says they "think it a pretty air castle to talk of the spiritual meaning of a ship or a cloud, of a city or a contract."

Hawthorne: But he did not believe in your correspondences.

George: But he did, Mr. Hawthorne. Read that wonderful prose poem, entitled "The Poet." He says therein, "The highest minds of the world have never ceased to explore the double meaning, or, shall I say, the quadruple, or the centuple, or much more manifold meaning of every sensuous fact."

Hawthorne (laughing): Ah, well, George, mystics and poets are alike to me. They see in a light by which I am dazzled.

Rivers: What! Do you acknowledge and illustrate our correspondence of the eye? "*They see.*" With what do they see? With their understandings, I suppose. "*In a light.*" What light? Truth, I suppose, is their lamp. "*By which I am dazzled.*" The fierce light of Truth, by which poets and mystics discern, dazzles your weaker intellect.

Hawthorne: Capital. I confess I am convicted. The correspondence of the eye is indisputable, and the passages you have quoted to confirm it remarkable.

George: There are ma' and Edith actually ready. What a lovely morning! We will go forth in the spirit of Wordsworth, not to moralize or argue, but to drink in the forces of Nature—

> "The eye, it cannot choose but see,
>   We cannot bid the ear be still;
> Our bodies feel where'er we be,
>   Against or with our will."

So let us see for one day, Mr. Hawthorne, whether we

cannot grow on Nature's own food held out from her own hands without our asking or seeking. Cannot we feed this "mind of ours in a wise passiveness" now and then?

Rivers: Well, George, I don't exactly know what Wordsworth means, but it is written, "Ask and ye shall receive; seek and ye shall find." We must go on asking and seeking if we want to be filled.

INTERLUDE VI.

"WHAT SHALL WE DRINK?"

THE little party had determined upon an excursion and a picnic, and when the ladies appeared at the close of the last conversation there was considerable hurry and bustle in getting off. Their drive lay through a pleasant and beautiful part of the country. The lanes were shadowed and overarched by long rows of trees, so that in parts our friends appeared to be moving along a grand cathedral nave of natural architecture, through the living pillars of which the sun glimmered down on graceful ferns and bending flowers. Through the breaks in the natural walls of living green, glimpses of wide stretches of country might be discerned, exhibiting every shade of verdure. Hawthorne was delighted, and loud in his praises of the landscape. Edith was charmed, and talked incessantly. Mrs. Rivers looked on all with that quiet joy which finds its best expression in silence. Mr. Rivers was meditative and thoughtful, now and then answering the remarks of his friend Hawthorne, and smiling at Edith's enthusiastic chatter. George was on the box beside the coachman, oblivious to all that was going on behind him, and absorbed in some occupation of his own. The sky was blue above him, the earth green beneath, and the larks were melodious all around him, but he was no more conscious of these than of Edith's laughter, or Mr. Hawthorne's voluble discourse.

"Hullo, George," said Hawthorne, "what are you doing up there?"

"Upon my word," said Edith, "he has got one of his crazy poets; take it away from him, Mr. Rivers."

"Is that the way you 'feed your mind in a wise passiveness,' George?" asked his father.

"It's Tennyson's last, just out," said George, "and I cannot resist it; look here!'

Saying this he turned round and asked his father to show Mr. Hawthorne the lines marked. They were in *De Profundis.*

"Oh, that stupid thing," said Edith.

"Stupid!" said George, with a withering look.

"What are the lines?" asked Mr. Hawthorne.

"They relate to the birth of a child," said Rivers, "and are these:

> " ' Out of the deep, my child, out of the deep,
> From that true world within the world we see,
> Whereof our world is but the bounding shore.'

Very good, George; they illustrate one subject of our conversations. The 'true world' is the substantial world; the 'world we see,' its shadowy correspondence in nature. The eye and the ear come out of the 'true world' into the 'world we see.'"

"It is all mystical nonsense," said Edith, taking the book; "you shall not have it again, George."

"No," said Mr. Hawthorne; "remember, my boy, your

own doctrine, and see if you cannot grow on Nature's food for a few hours."

George laughed, submitted to the deprivation, and for the rest of the drive entered into the spirit of his companions, and shared their conversation. When the party arrived at the scene of their picnic there was much conviviality, and a protest by Mr. Rivers against the wine-bibbers for not adhering to purer drinks.

"Now, father," said George, "on this point I must emphatically dissent from you. I agree with your sentiment on flesh-eating, though I do not follow your practice, but I can neither agree with your sentiment or practice in the matter of wine. Do you think it possible that anything so beautiful to the sight, so sweet to the nostril, and so delicious to the palate as this glass of champagne, can be evil?"

"My boy," said Mr. Rivers, "you must not judge according to the external appearance, but according to the interior quality of a thing."

"Well, its interior quality is to delight, exhilarate, and fill the soul with a genial glow."

"Rather," said Mr. Rivers, "to intoxicate, fascinate, dazzle, delude, destroy."

"But," said Mr. Hawthorne, "Jesus drank wine. According to the account of the miracle at Cana, He even produced it."

"My position on this subject," said Mr. Rivers, "is the same as on the subject of flesh-eating. It is permitted to the Church to eat flesh and drink wine; but in the beginning it was not so. To the Edenic people no flesh and no wine were allowed; but the first references to these things are as permissions to Noah and his successors. While God *permits* their use, it would be better for us to aim at the higher state, and realize delight in what He *orders*. In Eden there were the fruits and the river, as told at the beginning of Genesis; and it is the same with the New Jerusalem, as told at the end of Revelation."

"But, dear Mr. Rivers," said Edith, "is it really wrong for me to touch with my lips this tempting fragrant drop?"

"Not if you can do it conscientiously," said Mr. Rivers, smiling.

"Well, she can surely conscientiously do what Jesus did," said George. "John the Baptist came neither eating nor drinking, that is to say, he was not a flesh-eater nor a wine-drinker; but Jesus came eating and drinking, that is to say, He was both a flesh-eater and a wine-drinker. What do you say to that?"

"Why, what I have said before, that these things are allowable. In ordinary matters Jesus observed the general habits of the people among whom He lived. So may we in this respect, and be without sin. But still there may be a better way. The fruits that delighted and nourished the people of the Edenic times are better than the bloody flesh of the shambles, and so the

> 'Inoffensive must, and meathes
> From many a berry,'

and the 'dulcet creams' from 'sweet kernels pressed,' that Milton speaks of, are better than the fiery drinks of these latter times. That is my contention, and that, too, is my practice. Beyond this I do not go. I have no right to condemn those who think and act otherwise."

"You are a temperate teetotaller," said Mr. Hawthorne; "the first I ever knew. Teetotallers are an intemperate

G

class of men. You don't even think it is your duty to abstain as an example to the drunkard?"

"Certainly not," said Mr. Rivers, smiling; "for if the drunkard has refused to follow your example in the matter of temperance, he would not have been likely to follow mine in the matter of abstinence."

"But have you not said, father, that wine corresponds with truth, and that as men drink wine angels drink truth? Is not truth their wine?"

"Well, George, pure wine corresponds with pure truth, the wine consisting of such drinks as Milton speaks of in paradise—'must and meathes' and 'dulcet creams.' Unleavened bread and unfermented wine correspond with pure goodness and truth, the genuine nourishment of the soul. Leavened bread and fermented wine correspond with goodness and truth evolved by conflict with evil and falsehood."

"But is there not something in your favourite author about the angels becoming intoxicated with too much truth? And, by the by, Browning says—

   ' You must know that a man gets drunk with Truth
    Stagnant inside him !'

Too much fermented wine produces drunkenness here, and too much truth the corresponding effect there."

"You are a little in error," said Mr. Rivers. "An angel may indeed get drunk with truth *stagnant* inside him, but that state is altogether different to the mad drunkenness of an evil spirit filled with the fermenting substances of the infernal regions, which are falsehoods conflicting with truths, and which are *active* inside him. The state of an angel who drinks too deeply of heavenly mysteries is a kind of stupor rather than an inebriation.

He gets more truth than he has the power to digest, and he is for a time bewildered and stupefied. The madness of the devils revelling over falsehood corresponds with the drunkenness produced by alcohol, while the bewilderment and perplexity of an angel at the vastness of God's mysteries corresponds with the bodily bewilderment and depression caused by the imbibition of too much sweet and delicate liquid."

"Upon my word," said Edith, "I cannot understand either of you any more than I can this stupid poem of Tennyson."

Saying this she produced the objectionable volume and began to mouth out of it the lines to which George had drawn attention, "Out of the deep, my child, out of the deep," when he interposed, and took it from her hands.

"Such works are not intended for novel-reading girls," said he. "Look here, Mr. Hawthorne, here is another proof that our poets regard spirit as substance, flesh as shadow—

" 'O dear spirit, half lost
In thine own shadow and this fleshly sign
That thou art thou.'

The substance of the soul is half lost in the shadow of the body in which it becomes clothed."

"It is very remarkable, George," said Mr. Rivers; "there really is a depth of spiritual truth in the bards of the nineteenth century which we cannot too much admire, and you make me ashamed that I know so little about them."

Their repast being now over, the conversation was directed to other topics, and presently, having packed away the fragments, they were engaged in wandering over the heath, and in gathering specimens of wild flowers to be dried as mementoes of their visit. Having enjoyed themselves among the heath and the broom and the furze, they prepared to depart. The drive home was even more lovely than their morning experience. The sober quietude of the evening, the golden glories of the west, the wild cadences of the birds, and the glimpses at various turns in the road of the ocean reflecting all the colours living along the clouds, formed an ever varying scene of beauty, and suggested themes for pleasant discourse.

It was not till later on in the evening, when the lamps were lighted and they had gathered together in their pleasant room looking out upon the sea,—Mrs. Rivers, as usual, silent at her work,—that any of the party thought of renewing the subject of their conversations. At a pause in the music which Edith and George had provided, Hawthorne interposed, and the ever-recurring theme was at once resumed.

CHAPTER X.

THE EAR.

Hawthorne: Well, Rivers, we finished our talk about the eye this morning, and the next point is the ear. What is the correspondence of the ear?

Rivers: The eye perceives light, the ear sound. Spiritual light is truth, and the organ which perceives that light is the understanding. Spiritual sound —

Edith: Excuse me, Mr. Rivers; but *is* there such a thing?

Rivers: Well, Edith, when John was in the spirit he heard angels sounding trumpets. Were those metal instruments and were those earthly sounds, think you?

Edith: I don't know that we want to think anything about it. All we have to do is to believe what is written.

George: Edith is one of those sweet disciples of whom the Lord spoke when He said, " Blessed are they which have not seen, and yet have believed." Some of us sceptical Thomases want to see before we believe.

Rivers: There is the sound as well as the light of Truth. There is the thunder as well as the lightning of the Word. The lightning we perceive with the spiritual eye, the thunder with the spiritual ear.

Hawthorne: What is the spiritual ear? I am more puzzled in this matter than I expected.

Rivers: The spiritual ear is the ear possessed by the dead.

Edith: The ear possessed by the dead!

Rivers: Certainly, Edith. Don't you know it is written, "The dead shall hear the voice of the Son of God, and they that hear shall live"? How can the dead hear a voice unless they have ears?

Edith: Oh, that is about the resurrection.

Rivers: Just so. The dead rise when they hear the voice of the Son of God. Now, the voice of the Son of God is Divine Truth. When Divine Truth penetrates the spiritual ear of the dead soul, and it hearkens to that truth, it rises,—that is, it is elevated. The spiritual ear that hearkens to God's voice is that mental faculty which receives the truth and obeys it. This faculty is what we call the will. The light of truth affects the Understanding and illumines it; the sound of truth affects the Will and bends it to obedience. While, therefore, the Eye corresponds with the Intelligence that comes from seeing, the Ear corresponds with the Obedience that comes from hearing the voice of the Word. What is meant when it is complained that Israel hearkened not to the words of God? Clearly it means that they were disobedient. The obedient will is the hearing ear, and the disobedient will is the deaf ear.

Hawthorne: It is hardly so clear as the correspondence of the eye. What is meant by the ear of God? How can that be associated with obedience? Whom does God obey?

Rivers: The Divine eye is the Divine perception from

Wisdom, the Infinite Intellect. The Divine ear is the Divine perception from Love, the Infinite Will. Thus the Psalmist prays (lxxi. 2), "Incline Thine ear unto me, and save me." When God's love is bent toward us, He inclines His ear. Thus again, "Hear me, O Lord, for Thy *loving-kindness* is good" (Ps. lxix. 16). God's will, which is all loving-kindness, hearkens to our prayers. Thus again Isaiah says (lix. 1), "Neither is His ear heavy that it cannot hear." This means that the Divine Will is ever quick to the cry of the penitent. So with man, the human *ear* corresponds with the human *will*, and the *hearing* with the ear corresponds with the *obedience* of the will. Thus the Lord said, "He that hath ears to hear, let him hear."

Edith : Of course He did, Mr. Rivers; but what is there in that? That was simply the Lord's way of calling attention to His remarks.

Rivers : I think otherwise, Edith. We read in Isa. lv. 3, "Incline your ear and come unto me : hear, and your soul shall live." Do you think that every one who just hears with his outward organ will have the blessing and live? When the Lord says, "Incline your ear," does He not mean, Bend your wills? When He says, "Hear, and your soul shall live," does He not mean, Obey, and you shall be saved?

Hawthorne : It certainly seems so.

Rivers : So Jesus said, "My sheep hear my voice." The Lord's sheep are His disciples. They are obedient to His precepts. Nothing can be plainer.

Edith : But what has all this to do with salvation? I suppose it is not necessary to know all these strange notions before we can be saved?

Rivers : Certainly not, Edith.   But a knowledge of
the Word of God must be good and satisfying to the
soul as well as calculated to aid its growth in intelligence.
Do you remember the strange law among the Israelites,
that a servant who declined to go out free at the seventh
year of his servitude was to be brought to the door or to
the door-post, and his master was to bore his ear through
with an awl, and he was to serve for ever?

Edith : Who minds what strange things the Jews did?

Rivers : But this was expressly commanded by God.
To bring the willing servant to the door was representative of the bringing of the willing disciple to the Lord,
who, as to His Divine Humanity, is the means of entrance
to heaven.   He said, "I am the door."   The piercing
the ear through with an awl is representative of the
servant's will being pierced and affixed to the Lord.
Therefore it is added that he should serve for ever,
which signifies willing obedience to eternity.   You look
incredulous, Edith.   If your teachers would sometimes
condescend to remember that the Book of Exodus is just
as important as the Epistle to the Romans, you would
understand more about these things.   These words are
not those of Paul, but of God.   If Paul wrote of spiritual
things, much more did the Maker of this universe speak
of them.   The ceremony arose from the correspondence
of the Ear.

Hawthorne : The circumstance is noteworthy.   It is
not a little remarkable that so trivial a matter should be
represented as having been expressly commanded by the
Almighty.

Rivers : Again, in the ceremony of the Consecration,
the blood of the ram was to be placed upon the tip of

the right ear of Aaron and his sons. The blood, as you know, signifies Divine Truth, and the blood was put on the tip of the right ear because the right ear signifies the will of love, and Divine Truth affects the will of love with obedience. But I am afraid I am tiring you with these illustrations. I will just trouble you with one more. It is in Ps. xl. 6. The Psalmist says, "Mine ears Thou hast opened." What ears? Not those of his body, but those of his soul.

Edith : How *can* the soul have ears, Mr. Rivers?

George : Then I wonder of what use your harps will be, Edith.

Rivers : In the spiritual world the spiritual body will be furnished with organs of sense—eyes to see and ears to hear.

George : If you haven't eyes, Edith, you won't be able to see your own golden crown?

Edith : Now, George, you are really profane to talk in that way. The Scriptures say nothing about spiritual eyes and spiritual ears, and we have no right to argue about such things.

George : If the dead have no spiritual ears, I cannot understand how the good can hear, "Come, ye blessed," or the wicked, "Depart, ye cursed."

Rivers : That would be a strange state of existence in which we had no eyes nor ears. To be everlastingly blind and deaf would be no paradise. But, Edith, that you are wrong is very clear from the fact that it is written (Rev. vii. 17), "God shall wipe away all tears from their eyes." How could that be if spirits had no eyes? Again, do you remember how often it is enjoined, "He that hath an ear let him hear what the Spirit saith unto the

Churches"? The voice of the Spirit affects the spiritual and not the natural ear. The truth is, my dear, your teachers have taught you the language of a carnal religion. Your whole thought is concentrated on the material organs of the body, and you have never been taught that the invisible spirit is an organized spiritual substance, having spiritual organs invisible to natural sight, but clear and distinct to that of the spirit. If you read about the voices in the Book of Revelation, and of the hearing of the voices by the inhabitants of the world into which John was admitted when he was in the Spirit, you will easily see, Edith, that the just in heaven have ears, and that they are enabled therewith to discern the celestial harmonies.

Edith : Thank you, Mr. Rivers, I am sure ; you will be telling me next that we shall have noses in heaven.

This last remark, uttered with a pert jerk of the head, was too much for the gravity of the little party. A smile lighted up every one of their faces, while Mrs. Rivers looked up from her work and quietly remarked that she did not think any one would like to miss the celestial perfumes.

CHAPTER XI.

THE NOSTRILS.

Rivers : My dear Edith, you seem to be totally unaware that we can have no kind of human existence if we have no sensation. If we had no sense, but only life, in what way should we differ from a vegetable? The lowest animals have sensation, and you must be sure that the highest existences have it in highest perfection. The angels have eyes to see the beauty of the Lord their God. They have ears to hear the music of the eternal spheres. They have also nostrils with which they perceive the sweet odours exhaled from the flowers of Paradise, and through which they breathe the breath of Almighty God.

Edith (satirically): Please, Mr. Rivers, what are the flowers of Paradise?

Rivers (laughing): Such sweet souls as yours, Edith.

George : Yes; infantile and innocent spirits:

> " My Lord hath need of these flow'rets gay,
>   The Reaper said, and smiled :
> Dear tokens of the earth are they,
>   Where He was once a child."

Unfortunately some of the sweetest flowers are covered with prickles.

Rivers : Be quiet, George. By our natural senses we perceive the things of nature ; and can we doubt that we have spiritual senses by which we perceive the things of the spirit ? The great mischief in these days is wrought by the fact that your religious teachers, Edith, allow you to think that when the body is laid in the grave, the man is laid there. It follows from such teaching that when the organs of sense are buried the sense itself is destroyed. But behind the natural eye, ear, and nose, are the spiritual eye, ear, and nose, which cannot be buried, but which the man retains for the new state into which he enters. Now, that we have spiritual nostrils in heaven is clear from the odours that are spoken of as prevailing in that world. What is an odour without the nostril? Without the nostril there could be no such things as odours.

George : Besides, Edith, we read of the inhabitants of the spiritual world having eyes and ears, as we have learned ; and we read about their foreheads, on which names were written ; and of their mouths, out of which voices proceeded ; and of their faces, on which they fell : but what sort of faces would they be which had foreheads, eyes, ears, and mouths, but no noses?

Edith : Now, George, don't be ridiculous. You are only talking about the Book of Revelation, which was all a vision and nothing else.

Hawthorne : Never mind, Edith ; according to your own views it is a part of the Word of God, and you cannot ignore it. What is the correspondence of the nostrils, Rivers?

Rivers : By the natural nostrils we discern natural odours, and by the spiritual nostrils spiritual odours.

We certainly have some mental perception by which we discern the sweetness that exhales from the good, and the stench that exhales from the wicked. Now this mental perception constitutes our spiritual nose. We read of the Divine Nostrils. They are the Infinite Perceptions of the sweetness of justice, mercy, and humility exhaled from the human soul. Thus, when Noah offered his sacrifice after coming out of the ark (Gen. viii. 21), it is said the Lord smelled a sweet savour; and again, in the institution of the burnt-offering of the herd (Lev. i. 9), it is said to be "a burnt sacrifice, an offering made by fire, of a sweet savour unto the Lord." Now, these sacrifices typified those of which the apostle spake,—spiritual sacrifices, the offering of our daily duties,—and which are as sweet fragrances in the perceptions of our Heavenly Father.

Hawthorne: But we read of the breath of God's nostrils.

Rivers: Yes. The nostrils have two uses—they are for respiration as well as for the perception of odours. In this respect the Lord's nostrils correspond with Heaven, through which God breathes life into the Church on earth.

Hawthorne: Indeed!

Rivers: Certainly. The nostrils are a medium by which the breath of the body goes forth; they therefore correspond with the medium by which the breath of Jehovah—that is, Divine Truth—goes forth to give life to us. That medium is heaven. God's life is received in heaven by the angels, and mediately through the angels by us. You remember that Jesus breathed on His disciples, and said, "Receive ye the Holy Spirit" (John

xx. 22). In this relationship, therefore, the Divine Humanity or personality of Jesus corresponds with the Infinite Nostrils, because it is the medium for the diffusion of the Holy Breath or Spirit. Inasmuch also as the Divine Truth is breathed into us through the medium of the Word, the Word corresponds with the Divine Nostrils. Without Heaven, the Divine Humanity, or the Word, God could not breathe into our nostrils the breath of life, and we could not become living souls.

Hawthorne: You are now taking a high flight indeed —so high that I can hardly watch your progress.

Rivers: The subject is very simple. The laws of correspondence are grounded in the nature of uses. The use of the nostrils is, first, to perceive perfumes; next, to respire. Now in relation to God the nostrils correspond, first, with what we must all acknowledge our Heavenly Father to possess,—the power to perceive what is sweet and what is foul in human life. The sweet things are those associated with the love of our neighbour; the foul things are those associated with the love of ourselves. The former are to the Lord sweet smelling savours, and the latter offensive stenches. Is that clear?

Hawthorne: Perfectly so.

Rivers: In relation to God we read of His breathing out from His nostrils. This must refer to the outpouring of His life. His life is Truth. His truth is poured forth through God's ministering Spirits into our spirits. Consider that "spirit" signifies "breath," and thus that God's ministering Spirits are God's Breathers, and hence God's Nostrils, through which the life or truth of heaven pours. His truth also is outbreathed from His Human Nature in the person of Christ, and from His Word;

and thus these two correspond, in the supreme sense, with the nostrils. Is this plain?

Hawthorne : Yes, so far. But what about the destruction wrought by the breath of Jehovah's nostrils? Do we not read of such things in the Scriptures? Does Truth destroy? Is Heaven and the Word of God the medium through which evil comes like a blast upon the earth?

Rivers : The question is a very natural one. There are several passages of the kind you mention. In the Book of Job it is written concerning the wicked (iv. 9) : " By the blast of God they perish, and by the breath of His nostrils are they consumed." The truth breathed from heaven is one thing to the good and another to the evil. It is a soft air that revives the humble soul, but a blast that consumes the lofty mind. " Blessed are the meek " is a breath of God's nostrils that is like a gale of spring to the flowers of Christian lowliness, but like a Borean blast to the selfish growths of the proud heart.

Hawthorne : Ah, I understand. I ought to have known all that.

Rivers : Thus, in Ps. xviii. 15, it is written, " The foundations of the world were discovered at Thy rebuke, O Lord, at the blast of the breath of Thy nostrils." Divine Truth from heaven unveils the depths of things. It strips off appearances and discovers the foundations of evil. So in other places. Thus, then, you may remember that *any* medium or channel through which the Divine Truth is breathed on man corresponds with the nostrils of Jehovah.

Hawthorne : The science grows and developes. It is not so difficult of study as I thought. It is interesting, if not absolutely true.

Rivers : Then with respect to man's nostrils. They correspond first with the power of perceiving the sweetness or disagreeableness of the spiritual spheres exhaled from our neighbours. There are odorous and inodorous lives. The perfume of the heart is from God.

George : You remind me, father, of some beautiful lines :

> " Doubtless neither star nor flower
> Hath the power
> Such a sweetness to impart !
> Only God who gives perfumes,
> Flesh assumes,
> And with it perfumes my heart."

The spiritual nostrils alone can detect these perfumes.

Edith : Dear me ! I wonder you have been quiet so long. What is the name of the musty author ?

George : His name is George Herbert. I should have thought with your professions, Edith, you might have read his works. They are worth your study. I remember some other lines of his.

Edith : And of twenty other frowsy bards, I suppose.

George : No ; some other lines of George Herbert applicable to our subject, as showing that there are spiritual fragrances. Thus, speaking of the words " My Master," he says :

> "With these all day I do *perfume* my *mind*,
> My mind e'en thrust into them both ;
> That I might find
> What cordials make this curious broth,
> This broth of smells that feeds and fats my mind."

Edith (laughing) : We have that precious quotation over again ! A broth ! a broth of smells ! Who ever heard of such a thing?

George : Yes, Edith, a broth or compound of smells.

Hawthorne : Hush, Edith. You confuse the subject. George is quite right with these illustrations. There is a kind of poetical language in which the mind is shown as analogous to the body. The mind is fed and fattened and is delighted with smells. These are poetical figures, and I must say they assist our inquiry.

Rivers : Especially is the suggestion contained in the first verse quoted by George good. God perfumes our hearts with His flesh. His flesh is goodness, and this gives sweetness to the Christian soul. Now, as I have said, we all have the power to discern these sweetnesses in others. This perceptive power corresponds with the nostrils. Because it is possessed by God and us, so much is written about incenses in the books of the Law and in the Revelation. The elders in heaven are said to have vials full of odours which are the prayers of saints (Rev. v. 8). The vials full of odours signify the heart full of sweet things—sweet emotions and desires, which, you know, the poet says are prayers.

Edith : Not till they are put into words.

Rivers : Prayers are the soul's sincere desires, we are told, whether they are unuttered or expressed. Now we can discern these "sincere desires" in others, and are pleased therewith, because they affect us with a kind of fragrance. That in us which is affected is the spiritual nostril. Then, we have the power to inhale the breath of the Spirit. It is said in Gen. ii. 7, that God "breathed into his nostrils the breath of life, and man became a living soul." It does not mean that God breathed into man's natural nostrils the natural atmosphere and he became a living body. Mark what is treated of—God's

H

breathing; the breath of life, not atmospheric air; a living soul, not a living body. The nostrils which receive God's breath to make us alive must be spiritual. It is the power of reception of the Holy Breath breathed on us out of heaven by Jesus and from the Word. We have such power, and with this power the nostrils correspond.

Hawthorne : So you see, Edith, after all, our faces will be complete in the spiritual world. In addition to eyes, ears, forehead, and mouth, we shall have noses to make all symmetrical. I am half inclined to believe in this strange philosophy. It is so different to your know-nothing orthodoxy. Your teachers have a Bible full of marvellous things, and yet they seem to have studied nothing but a few chapters of the Apostle Paul. I shall have to begin to investigate Christianity *de novo.*

Edith : Well, do, pa'; I am sure I would rather have you believe as Mr. Rivers does, even if you made yourself stupid, as some other people, with poring over a lot of dreary poets, than have no religion at all.

George : Ah, you see, Edith has got the golden vial full of odours, though she doesn't often let one of them escape.

INTERLUDE VII.

"WHEREWITHAL SHALL WE BE CLOTHED?"

THE conversations which we have recorded in the previous chapters occupied the attention of our little party until it was time for them to retire. The three gentlemen were up early the next morning in order that they might get a breath of fresh air upon the beach. The salt sparkle of the sea and the brisk breeze that blew upon the shore were refreshing and health-inspiring, and seemed at once to enliven the blood and quicken the mind. A number of pleasure-boats were dancing about upon the waves, and several persons were enjoying an early bath. The scene was full of life, and our friends felt that it was a blessing only to live.

" By the bye," said Hawthorne, watching the swimmers rolling in the spray, " what would you do for clothes, Rivers, if every one carried out your views, and ate no flesh? What should we do for leather and wool?"

" We need not be wholly without these useful commodities," said Rivers; " we don't eat horses, and yet we have the opportunity of using their hides. So with oxen and sheep. We should find them useful without destroying them, and when it became necessary to take their lives, we could do as we pleased with their carcases. But, of course, leather and wool would not be so abundant. I think it probable that to answer our needs the vegetable kingdom would be found to contain all we required."

"Ah, you don't advocate a return to paradisal habits in that matter. We should eat and drink like the Edenites; but I suppose you would not have us adopt their practice in the matter of dress?"

Hawthorne and George laughed at what they anticipated a discomfiture for Rivers.

"Well," said he, "we cannot get back the innocence of Eden, although we may with profit emulate its simplicity in our food."

"Yes," said Hawthorne, "I suppose we must clothe ourselves while we are in this world; and I am afraid, when your theory is realized, and we find ourselves naked in our spiritual bodies in the spiritual world, we shall feel a bit ashamed."

"But what makes you think we shall be naked in the spiritual world?" asked Rivers.

"Why, if *we* are immortal, I don't suppose our *clothes* are," said Hawthorne, laughing.

"Have you considered," asked Rivers, "that those who have been seen in the spiritual world are described as being clothed?"

"I have not thought anything about it. I have, however, always considered it especially ludicrous that Hamlet's father's ghost should have been clothed in all his warlike gear, and also that every ghost story is associated with grey or white robes, and some of the apparitions are represented as wearing the very dress the deceased persons wore while alive."

"I pay no particular regard to popular ghost stories," said Rivers, "although I fully believe there have been spiritual appearances ; witness the case of Lord Brougham and his friend.[1] I simply draw your attention to the fact set forth in the Bible. There we learn that spiritual beings are clothed. The angels at the Lord's tomb were seen in shining garments. The elders, and those who came out of great tribulation, as spoken of in the Revelation, had white robes."

"But all that, I suppose, is figurative," said Hawthorne.

"I suppose it is," replied Rivers ; "but it is spoken of as a sensuous appearance notwithstanding. In the spiritual world we are clothed with honour or dishonour, with purity or impurity, according to our inward states.

---

[1] See "Life and Times of Lord Brougham," written by himself, vol. i. pp. 201-3. Lord Brougham had made a compact with a young friend whom he calls G——, and they had *written it in their blood*, to the effect that whichever of them died first should appear to the other. When Brougham was travelling in Denmark in 1799, the compact with his friend G—— having been entirely forgotten, and G—— himself having gone to India, he was taking a warm bath, and, he says, while lying in it and enjoying the heat, "I turned my head looking towards the chair on which I had deposited my clothes, as I was about to get out of my bath. On the chair sat G—— calmly looking at me. How I got out of the bath I know not, but on recovering my senses I found myself sprawling on the floor. The apparition, or whatever it was that had taken the likeness of G——, had disappeared." This was on the 19th December, and Brougham made a note of the fact. Soon after his return to Edinburgh he received a letter announcing G——'s death, and that he had died on the 19th December. Brougham thinks this must have been a dream, and his friend's death a coincidence. Such is the scepticism concerning the existence of a spiritual world and the possibility of its inhabitants making themselves visible, although it is one of the commonplaces of the Bible.

Here the robes of honour are worn by dishonourable men; there it will not be so. The interior there will clothe itself with a corresponding exterior. If our spiritual bodies be composed of the substance of goodness and truth, we shall be clothed with pure robes; but if they be composed of evil and falsehood, we shall be clothed with the rotten rags of impurity. This is an everlasting law which knows no variation."

"Indeed!" said Hawthorne; "do you mean to say that spirits have dresses and wardrobes and so forth?"

"Why not?" said Rivers. "The spiritual world is a world of substances. Spirits have robes for various occasions, and, I assume, places in which to keep them, even as we have in this world."

"Well, this surpasses all that I ever dreamed any man would be wild enough to set forth."

"That is because all your ideas have been, like those of the Church at the present day, materialistic. You have been thinking of the spiritual world as of a vacuity of shadows. It is the home of real men and women with wants corresponding with those they had in this world. That is why so much was made of the garments of Aaron and the priests and the ordinary Jew. God prescribed the character and pattern of those garments because they were to correspond with the character and pattern of those spiritual principles, which are really substances, that we are to wear in practice here, and that will be our real clothing after death."

"And do you say that we shall be able to take off one suit and put on another?"

"Yes, my dear friend, just as easily as we in this world put on a ceremonious behaviour for public occasions, and take it off and put on a familiar behaviour among our intimate acquaintances."

"Ah, I have a faint idea of your view. The dress will correspond with our moods of thought and action, and be changed with those moods?"

"Yes. Because dress corresponds with the conduct we assume before our neighbours, and because in the good that conduct is pure, the angels are robed in white garments. For the same reason we read of the 'defiled garment,' which corresponds with a defiled life, that is, depraved conduct. So with the 'wedding garment,' which the obtrusive guest had not on. The 'wedding garment' is the life or conduct that indicates oneness with the Lord."

"I like the view," said Hawthorne; "it is at least pretty, even if it be not true."

The discussion of the friends was interrupted by their arrival at their lodgings, where Mrs. Rivers and Edith were awaiting their return to breakfast. Hawthorne's mind, however, was seething with the subject, and it was not long before he took the opportunity to reintroduce the old theme.

CHAPTER XII.

THE TONGUE—TASTE.

Hawthorne: It is a fine taste that of yours, Rivers— biscuits and marmalade, rolls and butter, fruits and jams. I wish I could imitate it. Stronger flavours, you see, are more in my line.

Edith: And in mine!

Rivers: So I see, Edith. But while you eat your lamb chop, have you no vision of the bleating innocent under the butcher's hands?

Edith: Dear me, Mr. Rivers, Jesus ate of the paschal lamb!

Rivers: Yes. He fulfilled all the Law, and therefore ate of the Passover.

Hawthorne: By the bye, Rivers, we see, hear, and smell in the spiritual world; do we taste also?

Rivers: Undoubtedly. The Scriptures distinctly mention facts which prove it. John, the beloved apostle, when in the spirit was made to experience it. He ate a little book.

Edith: Really, Mr. Rivers, is it not absurd? All that was only a kind of dream. How can a book be really eaten?

George: Why, Edith, I have seen you really devour three volumes in a day!

Edith : And I have seen you chewing over a tough bit of a poem half-a-dozen times without being able to digest it.

Rivers (laughing) : Well, Edith, you have helped my illustration quite as well as George. You devour volumes; George chews over indigestible poems; and John ate a book. Now, he ate this book when he was in the spirit, and thus it was a spiritual operation. When you devour your novels, you find some pages dry as mouldy crusts ; some as delicious and juicy as ripe peaches. When George studies the poets, he finds some of their lines tough and some tender. John found the book in one respect sweet, and in another bitter. How could a book be found either bitter or sweet unless we had a spiritual palate, and with it the sense of taste ?

Hawthorne : To eat a book, according to your idea, is to make yourself acquainted with its contents?

Rivers : We read in the Scriptures of spiritual hunger and thirst. There are the hunger and thirst after righteousness. " My soul thirsteth for God,". says the Psalmist. Now it must be obvious that spiritual hunger and thirst are mental appetites, desires, affections. He who has an affection or desire for righteousness, hungers and thirsts for it. When the thing that we desire is obtained and taken into the mind, it is eaten. Spiritual eating, therefore, is internal reception and appropriation. When we have a desire for anything, and internally appropriate it, it affects us with delight, satisfaction, disappointment, or disgust, according to our spiritual palate. Thus to eat the book, as described in Rev. x. 10, is to put the goodness and truth which it contains into the spiritual mouth.

Edith : Spiritual mouth !

George: Certainly. What would thirst be without a mouth and a dry tongue in it? We speak of drinking in the truth. How can truth be drunken without a suitable mouth?

Rivers (smiling): Or goodness eaten? Look, in your leisure, at Isa. lv. 1, 2: "Hearken diligently unto me, and eat ye good, and let your soul delight itself in fatness." You will see in those two verses that both eating and drinking are spoken of in relation to spiritual things, and that implies a mouth and a palate. Again, " Open thy mouth wide, I will fill it." Goodness and truth first enter the spiritual mouth, and then they are conveyed into the spiritual stomach. The mouth is the memory into which knowledge is first received, and the stomach the rational faculty where it is digested. The book was sweet in the mouth, but bitter in the belly. Truth is sweet to us often when it is mere knowledge in the memory, but it is bitter when it has to be pondered over and digested inwardly, as it then begins to come into contact with the evil life of our spiritual system.

Hawthorne: I perceive the idea very clearly. When we read a book, we are eating and tasting it. The correspondence of taste, therefore, is with the delight or undelight with which knowledge affects us.

Rivers: Yes. The tongue is the principal organ of taste, and in this respect it corresponds with the affection for goodness and truth, or their opposites evil and falsehood. The taste corresponds with the perception of the quality of goodness and truth according to our states. Thus, in certain states of the body, things which when we are in health are pleasant to the tongue become unpleasant. So to a healthy affection goodness and truth are sweet; to an unhealthy one, bitter.

Hawthorne: The analogies are so far perfect.

Rivers: They are true correspondences. There cannot be a single thing in the body without something corresponding thereto in the spirit. All the numerous nerves and papillæ of the tongue have their correspondences in the soul, the latter being the hidden causes, the former the manifested effects. Now, that the tongue corresponds with the affection of knowledge, we may know from the wonderful narrative in the seventh chapter of Judges, where we are told that God instructed Gideon to bring his army to the brook, and to go against Midian with the three hundred who lapped the water with the tongue as a dog lappeth it. The three hundred overthrew the Midianites. This is a parable. The Tongue lapping the Water is the Affection eagerly lapping Knowledge. By those who have such spiritual tongues the hosts of Falsehood are overthrown.

Hawthorne (musing): We eat goodness and drink truth and taste their flavours.

Rivers: Briefly, the correspondence of the taste is recognised in the Word of God, and many illustrations of it may be given. Take for instance Ps. cxix. 103: "How sweet are Thy words to my taste! yea, sweeter than honey to my mouth!" The Lord's words are said to be sweet to the taste, or palate as it is in the Hebrew. What can this mean? It means that Heavenly Truth is agreeable to the good man's Affection. This affection is therefore our spiritual palate. Again, in Jer. xv. 16: "Thy words were found, and I did eat them; and Thy word was unto me the joy and rejoicing of my heart." The word is the Divine Goodness in the form of Divine Truth. It is eaten when it is received and appropriated in the mental system. It is the joy and rejoicing of the heart when it is sweet in that perception which is the spiritual tongue.

Hawthorne : I am more than satisfied on this point.

Edith : Well, pa', every one will admit there is something suggestive in all this as figures of speech, such as George can pick out of a thousand and one poets, but it cannot be anything more. No one can believe that there are eating and drinking in heaven, for that would be to make it just like this world.

Rivers : Well, if nobody can believe that there are eating and drinking in heaven, then nobody can believe the Lord's own words. Does He not say, "I appoint unto you a kingdom, as my Father hath appointed unto me, that ye may eat and drink at my table in my kingdom ?" (Luke xxii. 29, 30).

Edith : Dear me, Mr. Rivers, surely you will not say that there are tables there ?

Rivers : Certainly. We have spiritual tables here on which spiritual bread and wine are spread, and whence we may take them. The Word of God is a spiritual table laden with spiritual dainties to feed and delight us. The Word of God is in heaven, and it is a Divine table in every home, laden with what the angels need to eat and drink. And again : "Blessed is he that shall eat bread in the kingdom of God." You see in the kingdom there will be the eating of bread, that is, the reception of the Divine Goodness.

Edith : Well, it is of no use talking if you spiritualize the whole Bible away in that manner.

Hawthorne : My dear child, I am sorry you are so obtuse. What do you mean by "spiritualize *away ?*"

It is quite evident that you have nothing to lose, for you had no idea respecting that declaration that the Lord's disciples should eat and drink at His table or eat bread in His kingdom. You must possess some view of it before it can be taken or spiritualized *away*. I confess, so far as I am concerned, that Mr. Rivers has taken nothing away but given something. He has been trying to spiritualize the Word for me into existence.

Edith : I am glad of it, pa' ; but we must all have our own way of looking at things.

Hawthorne : But you, Edith, really don't seem to look at them at all. They are out of view. You know nothing of such matters, and, when an effort is made to place them before you, you say they are taken away. I say that Mr. Rivers has for me spiritualized the Word into existence, and if you were not pre-occupied with your know-nothing notions about religion and the Bible, it would have been spiritualized· *into* your hands instead of *out* of them.

Edith : Oh, thank you, pa' ; and you too, George—I understand your looks.

Mrs. Rivers : Edith believes far more than you give her credit for.

Rivers : I am sure she does. I believe she has tasted the spiritual food offered at these little banquets of ours, and that she is not wholly displeased with its flavour.

CHAPTER XIII.

THE SKIN—TOUCH.

Hawthorne: There is yet one sense of which we have said nothing. If spirits have the sense of taste, of course they must have that of touch.

Edith: I am not so sure of that. We cannot touch spirits, nor can spirits touch us. Who ever heard of such a thing?

Rivers: But though we cannot touch spirits, Edith, we can touch each other. So, though spirits cannot touch men on earth, I suppose it may be possible for them to touch kindred spirits in heaven.

George: What is taste but the result of touch? How could the Psalmist have said, " How sweet are thy words to my taste," if they had not touched his tongue? The sense of touch is implied in that of taste, of which we have already been speaking this morning.

Rivers: Quite true. Honey touching the tongue *communicates* its quality, sweetness. So iron and wool touching the skin *communicate* their qualities, hardness and softness, solidity and elasticity, to the hand. The quality of these things is translated to the skin. Thus Touch corresponds with mental Communication or

Translation. When one spirit's hand touches another's, their qualities are immediately and mutually known because the touch is harsh or agreeable according to their congenial or uncongenial states. There is warmth in the touch of a charitable hand in the spiritual world, and chilliness in that of an uncharitable one. The warmth or chilliness is communicated or translated to those with whom it comes in contact. Hence the correspondence.

Hawthorne : The touch of bodies on earth corresponds with the contact of minds in the spiritual world?

Rivers : That is so. Because the Touch corresponds with Communication the Lord wrought many of His miracles by the touch. Nay, read the strange circumstance mentioned in Isa. vi. 5, 6, where the prophet is represented as saying, "Woe is me ! for I am undone ; because I am a man of unclean lips," when one of the seraphims, having a live coal from the altar, laid it upon his mouth, and said, "Lo, this hath touched thy lips ; and thine iniquity is taken away, and thy sin purged." The live coal from the altar represents the fire of living love from heaven. Its touching the lips signifies the communication of that fire to the life, seeing that love alone takes away iniquity and purges us of sin. Again, in Jer. (i. 9), the prophet says the Lord touched his mouth, and said, "Behold, I have put my words in thy mouth." Touching the mouth here evidently means communication of the Truth or Word of heaven. Once more, the Lord Jesus touched the leper and cleansed him, the hand of Peter's wife's mother and cured her of the fever, the eyes of the blind and opened them, the smitten ear and healed it. The touch of the Lord Jesus signifies the communication of His life or quality in which is health and strength. I might give you some dozens of illustrations of the correspondence of touch. The touch of material bodies, which is the contact of flesh and blood through the skin, corresponds with the touch of spirits, which is the contact of their charity and faith through the sphere of life by which they are encompassed.

Hawthorne: As I said, therefore, touch really corresponds with mental contact.

Rivers: Yes. Thus, those who are sundered in body may touch as to their souls, and I am not sure that there are not well-authenticated instances in which such things have occurred in the experience of persons on earth. But let that be. Touch corresponds with mental contact and all that it involves. There cannot be a contact of mind without a communication of thought and affection, and thus you will see that touch really corresponds with mental communication. Thus, not only are there the cases to which I have referred you in the Scriptures, but there are others of equal moment. Consider the observances enjoined upon the Jews. Every one who touched the things of the tabernacle and of the sacrifices was holy. That was because it shadowed forth the communication of holiness from the holy things of heaven to the soul in contact therewith. Can you imagine that God would have ordained such a thing unless something spiritual had been involved in it?

Hawthorne: Well, I certainly cannot.

Rivers: But, still more remarkable, those who touched unclean things were unclean. He who touched a dead body was unclean seven days. Every one who touched a bone or sepulchre was unclean. Every one who touched an unclean person, or an unclean beast, was unclean until the evening. All this was because the law of representatives prevailed in that Church of types and shadows. Evils as well as goodnesses communicate themselves when we come in contact with them, and this fact is foreshadowed in these Jewish laws.

Hawthorne: It appears to me that touch is concerned more or less with every sense. As George has remarked, taste results from touch, and is in reality a form of touch. Taste is the sensation produced by touch on the tongue. So with the sense of smell. It results from the touch of odoriferous particles upon the olfactory nerves. Hearing is the effect of certain vibrations touching the auditory nerves, while sight results from the touch of light in its various modifications upon the optic nerves. So if we deny touch to spirits, we must deny to them the possession of every other sense.

George: Taste is touch on the tongue; smell, touch on the nostrils; hearing, touch on the ear; and sight, touch on the eye. What do you say to that, Edith?

Edith: Of course; every one knows that. When our bodies rise, we shall have all these senses, I daresay, but not before. I never *will* believe that spirits have senses. How should they?

Rivers: Well, Edith, there is something in the Lord's parable about the rich man and Lazarus that should teach us in this matter. We are told that in hell the rich man lifted up his eyes, being in torment, and saw Lazarus in Abraham's bosom. He then asked for water to cool his tongue. Now here are three facts. The rich man had *eyes* and saw with them; he had a *tongue* and

I

could taste with it; he had sensitive nerves, and could be tormented. Moreover, Abraham spoke to him, and he heard what was said, for he made an answer. Thus it is plain that he had *ears* and heard with them. It is beyond doubt that the rich man was in possession of all his senses, although his body had not risen, for he is represented as having gone into the spiritual world immediately upon death.

Edith : Why, Mr. Rivers, you can make nothing of that. It is only a parable.

Rivers : Just so; but still, I suppose the lesson is taught by reference to actual things. Thus the sower and the seed, the woman and the leaven, the merchant-man and his pearls, are all parables; but the lesson is taught by reference to existing realities. The Lord would not have taught the parable of the woman and the leaven had there been no such things as women, meal, and leaven; and so he would not have taught the parable of Lazarus in Abraham's bosom and the rich man in hell had there not been such realities. Rely upon it, my dear, sight, hearing, smell, taste, and touch, are all faculties of the spirit and not of the body, and that it is the spirit that sensates through the body and not the body without the spirit.

George : Why, does not the spirit sensate in dreams? Do you remember Byron's paradox?—

> "Strange state of being! (for 'tis still to be)
> Senseless to feel, and with sealed eyes to see."

When all our natural senses are lapped in slumber, are not those of the spirit often in full activity? I remember Sir Thomas Browne says, "In one dream I can compose a whole comedy, behold the action, apprehend the jests, and laugh myself awake at the conceits thereof." How could you see things with your eyes shut if the soul had not the power of vision? Or how touch them, unless the soul had the power to feel?

Edith: But what we experience in dreams is only imagination. We don't really see and touch, we only imagine that we do so.

George (laughing): Yes. Some people hold that all is imagination, even in our waking state. You cannot, however, make common-sense people believe it. Suppose that while you were dreaming, somebody in your dream told you it was all fancy, and that you were not really seeing and hearing. Would you accept the statement?

Edith: Perhaps not.

George: No; you would repudiate it. You would maintain that your senses did not deceive you. You know what Tennyson says :—

" Dreams are true while they last, and do we not live in dreams?"

They are true while they last, because in them, without the use of the natural organs, the spirit really sensates.

Rivers: It is only on the theory that the spirit possesses the senses, that we can understand the Word of God at all. Isaiah, Jeremiah, Ezekiel, Daniel, Zechariah, had visions of God. How did they perceive them but by the exercise of the spiritual senses? They saw marvellous things never seen by earthly eye. How could they see them but by the heavenly eye? They heard wondrous voices unheard by earthly ears. How could that be except by the exercise of their inward ears? They felt the spirit touch them and lift them up. Ezekiel tasted the roll of the spiritual book, and it was in his mouth as honey for sweetness; and the same experience came upon John. We must ignore all this unless we accept the simple truth that the spirit has the power to sensate as well as to will and to think. The prophets did not merely *imagine* that they saw and heard ; they really *did* see and hear. It becomes a question of the credibility of the Word of God.

Hawthorne : Without sensation, existence is inconceivable. Imagine a man without the power to see, hear, smell, taste, or touch. What would he be? An animated block of marble, wanting in everything that constitutes humanity.

INTERLUDE VIII.

"DUST THOU ART, AND UNTO DUST SHALT THOU RETURN."

THE discussion was broken off when the little family rose from breakfast, and they had no opportunity for renewing it during the day. Hawthorne, however, was in a very remarkable state of mind, and he could not rest long without giving expression to some of his feelings. A severe blow had fallen upon the head of his scepticism. It was scotched, but not killed. He was, above all things, surprised to find that so much could be said for a book which he had absolutely despised as unphilosophical and unscientific. He was always, therefore, anticipating a breakdown in the system which his friend had been developing, and he watched the process with interest as well as curiosity. The science of correspondences had astonished him beyond measure, because it was perfectly new, and also because it seemed to follow a definite law, which, however, he could not grasp, and elicited such extraordinary harmonies from the Scriptures. In the evening, therefore, when the friends found they had an hour's leisure, he renewed the topic.

"Come, Rivers," said he, "you speak of the spiritual

character of man. Does not the Bible itself acknowledge him to be nothing but matter?"

"Certainly not," said Rivers; "the whole Bible is founded on man's immortality and immateriality."

"Well, then," said Hawthorne, "what does it mean when it describes God as saying to Adam, 'Dust thou art, and unto dust shalt thou return'? Is not dust matter?"

"Ah, you see," said Rivers, "for want of a knowledge of correspondences you miss the spirituality of the declaration. The dust there is applied to the spirit."

"That is directly opposed to what Longfellow sings," said George. "He says—

'Dust thou art, to dust returnest,
    Was *not* spoken of the soul.'

It seems difficult to believe that dust has any relation to the spirit."

"To understand that expression you must understand the correspondence of dust," said Rivers. "But, first, let me ask you, Can a man—a thinking, loving subject— return to material dust? His *body* may; but *man* does not. If he is not immortal, he is annihilated at death. You remember what the Psalmist says, 'My soul cleaveth to the dust.' Do you suppose his mind clung to material dust?"

"Ah, I see," said Hawthorne, "you are going to spiritualize the passage *away*, as Edith would say."

"I don't know that I should say so, pa'," said Edith, who was unwilling to agree with either side.

"Dust," continued Rivers, "corresponds with that which is worthless and corrupting in relation to the spirit. Naturally speaking, in itself, dust is of no value. Nothing will grow in it. It is taken up by every wind, and fills our eyes, ears, nostrils, pollutes our very mouths, incrusts our skin—in fact, disturbs our every sense. Our selfishness, worldlinesses, sensualities, carnalities, are spiritual dust, and correspond with natural dust. Nothing good will grow in these things. No trees of righteousness can take root, blossom, and bear fruit in the loose dust of worldly thoughts and loves. Our spiritual sight and hearing are darkened and deafened by them, blown as they are into the spiritual eye and ear by every blast of error. They clog up our perceptions of the odours and flavours of heaven, and they incrust our lives so that we are no longer sensitive to the sweet soft touch of goodness. Do you see the correspondence?"

"You have traced it out with tolerable accuracy," said Hawthorne, "as I anticipated you would. But serpents don't eat carnalities, and all the rest of the things you mention, any more than they eat the dust of the earth," he added, smiling.

"No," said Rivers, "and that remark shows how the most attentive and intelligent have to be taught and retaught before they get clear views of this great subject. I remember my own experience in the matter."

"Why, pa'," said Edith, "you have forgotten that the serpent has its correspondence."

"Exquisite," said George; "we have at last won over the only person who never *would* believe anything reasonable!"

"Don't suppose that I believe a word of it," said Edith; "only I knew how Mr. Rivers would get out of it."

"Well, it's something," said Rivers, "only to see so far. It is said, 'Upon thy belly shalt thou go, and dust shalt thou eat all the days of thy life.' The serpent corresponds with man's serpentine nature, which is his sensual appetite. This, before the great sin, was high and noble. It was at first delighted with heavenly beauties and harmonies and sweetnesses. After the great sin it was degraded, and fed upon gross carnalities and worldlinesses, spiritual dust. So it is at the present day, according to the prophecy, 'Dust shall be the serpent's meat.'"

"Is that how you considered father would 'get out of it'?" said George; "perhaps, Edith, you will tell us how *you* would have got out of it. Natural serpents always went upon their bellies, and none of them will eat dust. Give us your explanation."

Edith looked indignant, and was silent.

"Now," continued Rivers, "when God said to the Man, 'Dust *thou* art,' He did not mean that his *body* was dust. God meant that Man in himself is mere carnality, worldliness, and selfishness. He is preserved from this by receiving the inbreathed Spirit of God. God breathed, it is said, into man's nostrils, and he became a living soul. When man sinned and departed from God, thus alienating himself from the Divine Spirit, he returned into himself, that is, into the carnality, worldliness, and selfishness which is his essential nature. Thus every man who now is taken by the Spirit of God out of his selfishness, is taken out of the dust, and if he quits the Spirit of God and returns into his selfishness, he returns to the dust. Thus, you see, my dear Hawthorne, we learn by this text something more about man than that he is composed of mere matter."

"I admit that much may be said for your view," said Hawthorne, "and I will not now contest it. Shall we proceed with our old theme, and carry it on a step further ?"

"By all means," said Rivers.

The little party then disposed themselves to consider a further development of the interesting point associated with the correspondence of the body and its several features.

CHAPTER XIV.

THE HEAD AND ITS FEATURES.

Hawthorne: As the body corresponds with the soul, and is, as you say, its image, I suppose every part of the body corresponds with some feature of the soul or some mental faculty.

Rivers: Certainly. Now, we have treated of the general components of the body—such as its flesh, blood, bones, etc.—suppose we consider some of those particular features to which you refer.

Hawthorne: I shall be delighted. There is the head, the trunk, the limbs.

Rivers: Yes, and their details and contents, such as the face—

Hawthorne: And the organs of speech.

Rivers: With the heart and the lungs.

Hawthorne: And do you say that they all have their special correspondence, and that this can be illustrated from the Scriptures?

Rivers: Most decidedly.

Hawthorne: I think it a very pretty air castle, beautiful in every detail, but standing on an insecure foundation. Men may have invented a system of symbols—in fact, there is a certain symbolic law according to which we all speak, and I think it possible that it has no other origin than the ingenuity of the human mind.

Rivers: Then all books whatever should be solvable by correspondences, and evolve hidden meanings. But this is not so. The sacred books are alone amenable to this system of interpretation.

Hawthorne: Well, what do you say to the correspondence of the Head?

Rivers: That the head of the body denotes a special faculty is obvious from Ps. cx. 7: "He shall drink of the brook in the way: therefore shall he lift up the head." The psalm is all about the Lord. Are you prepared to say that it refers to the drinking of natural water and to the lifting up of the natural head?

Hawthorne: Tell me your idea.

Rivers: The head is the highest part of the body, and also the noblest and most important. It therefore corresponds with that which is highest and noblest in the soul. Now that which is highest and noblest in the soul is that which is inmost. The head, therefore, corresponds with the INMOST FACULTY whence spiritual life and thought emanate as natural life and action emanate from the head. The inmost faculty of man is the Will, into which the Divine Life immediately flows, and which has eyes and ears and nostrils for all things beautiful and sweet, and a power of expression more complete than our outward vocal organs.

Hawthorne: Stay, let me understand. The Head corresponds with—what?

Rivers: The Will, where Love resides, with all those marvellous emanations corresponding with the organs

seated in the head. Now it is said in our psalm that
" He shall drink of the brook in the way : therefore shall
he lift up the head." To drink of the brook is to imbibe
Truth from its fountain; this elevates the Love, this
fortifies the Will, depressed by wandering in the mazy
ways of error.

Hawthorne : It is not a bad illustration.

Rivers : Then, of course, you remember Nebuchadnezzar's dream. He saw a great image, the head being
of gold, the breast of silver, the belly and thighs of
brass, and the legs and feet of iron and clay. That
suggests, by the various metals mentioned, the correspondence of the various parts of the body. The head
was of gold, because gold from its richness corresponds
with love, and love is of the inmost of the soul, the will.

Hawthorne : But it is said that Nebuchadnezzar himself was this head of gold.

Rivers : Oh, that is the mere historical interpretation
of the vision given in the letter of the chapter. I am
speaking of the spiritual interpretation, which is in the
spiritual sense. The head corresponds with the highest
things of heaven and of the human spirit. These are the
things of love in which alone is life. Hence the head
was of gold. This was the reason why Aaron and the
priests and the kings were consecrated by the pouring of
oil upon the head. Oil also signifies love, and this
sanctifies man's inmost or highest nature, the will, and
fits him for a priest and king before God. Hence, too,
in the book of Revelation, God's name is said to be in
the foreheads of His servants (xxii. 4). God's name is
His quality, which is Love, and this is impressed upon
the Will.

Hawthorne: The Will! I cannot quite understand it.

Rivers: Is not the head the will of the body? Does not the head move the body and its various parts? As the head wills, the body acts. So love in the soul wills, and thought, which is spirit action, follows. Love and will are synonymous, for what the spirit loves, that it wills. While the understanding is the receptacle of truth and exercises thought, the Will is the receptacle of goodness and exercises Love.

Hawthorne: I perceive the distinction.

Rivers: Then the Face is of the head, and corresponds with man's interior affections. The reason is, because the affection is written in the face, unless a man acts the hypocrite and tries to conceal it. We say in common conversation that the face is the index of the mind. Thus we read in the Scriptures so much about the Lord's face: "The Lord make His face shine upon thee." The Lord's face signifies the Divine interiors, which are mercy and love. These we need to shine into our souls. We read of seeking the face of the Lord, which signifies seeking the Divine Love. We read of the Lord hiding His face, which signifies withdrawing His love.

Hawthorne: What! Does the Lord withdraw His love from men?

Rivers: No, the Lord's face is hidden when men turn to evil, as it is written in Isaiah (lix. 2), "Your sins have hid His face from you." Thus we have many prayers in the Psalms for the light of the Lord's countenance, and that He will make His face shine upon the people. Thus (Ps. iv. 6), "Lord, lift Thou up the light of Thy countenance upon us;" and again (Ps. lxvii. 1), "God be merciful unto us, and bless us: and cause His face to shine upon us." The light of the Lord's countenance is the heavenly blessing that flows from the Infinite Love, and the shining of His Face is the expression of His Mercy and Beneficence.

Hawthorne: All that, of course, may be admitted. Indeed, it is perfectly obvious. Having the idea of God as of a man—for the anthropomorphic notion runs all through the Hebrew literature—it could not be otherwise expressed.

Rivers: The anthropomorphic notion is the true one, for no man can form any other than a human conception of God. If you get rid of the human idea you are lost in the vastness of the universe, and have nothing but a vague conception of a pervading force. Inasmuch as there cannot be force without a subject, you make nature itself subject as well as object, and thus the idea of God vanishes altogether. But the Scriptures present Him under an aspect conceivable and graspable, and represent Him as a Divine Man. It is the necessity of our weakness.

George: Ah, very forcibly expressed by Robert Browning. He makes David cry to Saul:

" 'Tis the weakness in strength that I cry for! my flesh that I seek
In the Godhead! I seek it and find it. O Saul, it shall be
A Face like my face that receives thee : a Man like to me
Thou shalt love and be loved by for ever! a Hand like this
  hand
Shall throw open the gates of new life to thee. See the Christ
  stand!"

Man cannot think above Humanity; hence the necessity for a Divine Humanity to enable him to think of God at all.

Rivers : Very good indeed, George. Thus God is everywhere described in the Scriptures as a Man and as having human features. We see it remarkably so in the first chapter of the Apocalypse. In the midst of the seven golden candlesticks was one like to the Son of Man. His head and hairs were white like wool; His eyes were like a flame of fire; out of His mouth went a sharp two-edged sword; and His countenance was as the sun shining in his strength. The Lord's head corresponds, as I have said, with the Infinite Will; the flaming eyes with the brilliancy of the Divine Intelligence and Foresight; the countenance shining as the sun in its strength with the fulness of the expression of the Divine Love. But the probability is that I have said more than you needed to hear to illustrate the subject.

Hawthorne : Your meaning is perfectly plain. So far as the descriptions of the Lord's face and its shining on man go, I can very well understand that they refer to the flowings forth of the Divine Goodness towards us.

Rivers : Well, that the Face of Man has relation to the Human Interiors which it expresses, you may know by one passage only: "The wicked through the pride of his countenance will not seek after God." Now, there is no pride in the countenance which is not first in the soul. It is the pride of man's love — of his interior affection — that keeps him from seeking after God, because it is fixed supremely upon itself!

Hawthorne : I may admit that too. In the incident you referred to out of the Apocalypse you said nothing about the sword going out of the mouth. The mouth is in the head, and must correspond, according to your theory, with something associated with it.   It is not a nice picture—a sword going out of the mouth.

Rivers : Perhaps not, but it is a true one.   What comes from the mouth of God is Truth, and it is sharp, and to that which is evil and false, like a sword, destructive. The Mouth, with the tongue and the lips, so far as it is used for speaking, corresponds with the Doctrine which expresses the truth.

Hawthorne : Why, you said the bones correspond with doctrine.

Rivers : So far as doctrine is *held* by us, and forms the framework and support of our religion.   But the mouth corresponds with doctrine so far as it is *taught* by us, whether by voice or life.

Hawthorne : " Open thy mouth wide : I will fill it." What does that mean ?

Rivers : The mouth has two uses.   One use is for the reception and mastication of food, another is for speech. Of course the correspondence is different.   The mouth in the passage you have quoted signifies the affection for knowledge, which is spiritual food.   But we are speaking of the latter use.   In that respect the mouth, the tongue, and the lips correspond with the *enunciation* of know-ledge, in the former case with the *affection* and *reception* of knowledge.   Now, that the mouth, with of course the tongue in it and the lips, signifies doctrine in the Scriptures, I will prove to you by one passage.   In Isaiah vi. 5 and the following verses, the prophet says, " Woe is me ! for I am undone ; because I am a man of unclean lips, and I dwell in the midst of a people of unclean lips : for mine eyes have seen the King, the Lord of hosts."   The prophet had seen the King,—his eyes had been opened to Truth,—and this led to the confession that he and the Israelites had unclean lips. He did not mean that their natural lips were soiled. Having a revelation of God, he saw the impurity of their doctrine,—that what they taught for truth was falsehood. Is that plain?

Hawthorne : I admit it.

Rivers : Well, the prophet goes on to say that one of the seraphims took a live coal off the altar and laid it upon his *mouth*, and said, "Lo, this has touched thy *lips ;* and thine iniquity is taken away, and thy sin purged." This being done, he was commissioned to go and teach the people. The live coal from the altar signifies the living love of God ; its touching the mouth and the lips signifies its touching his doctrine and communicating to it the heavenly heat. What else can you make of it ?

Hawthorne : I desire to make nothing else of it. The system holds together wondrous well. I suppose I shall find a weak part in it by and by.

Rivers : Now, you see, we have the faculties which have the same relation to the soul as the head and its organs have to the body. The optic, auditory, and olfactory nerves, as well as the facial and labial muscles, are all associated with the head. The head corresponds with the WILL, which is really the whole Man, and with the will are associated the spirits' eyes, ears, nostrils, countenance, mouth, and lips. The will discerns by its various faculties and expresses itself by its various mediums in just the same way as the head discerns and expresses itself by its various organs.

K

INTERLUDE IX.

"THEY NEITHER MARRY NOR ARE GIVEN IN MARRIAGE;
BUT ARE AS THE ANGELS OF HEAVEN."

OUR readers will not have guessed from the part assigned
to George and Edith in these conversations, that there
was any special tender relationship between them. The
fact is, the light banterings which we have from time to
time reported were only the ripplings on the surface of
a full deep stream of affection. Their apparent indiffer-
ence to each other's tastes was assumed, for in truth they
were both equally fond of the poets and the writers of
the higher class of fiction. To be sure, Edith had, as
we have said, received the ordinary orthodox notions of
religion, and knew very little of any other till these
conversations commenced, and throughout them she had
assumed an earnestness about her preconceptions which
she did not feel, and all the time had been an attentive
listener to Mr. Rivers' expositions.

One morning they had gone out for a ramble by
themselves, and had reached the top of some cliffs
looking far out to sea, and they had sat down to rest
themselves and enjoy at once the rich breeze and lovely
prospect.

"Now, George," said Edith, "don't quote poetry or I shall run away. You know I hate it."

"Yes," said he, "just as I hate Dickens, and Thackeray, and George Eliot, and Jane Eyre, and the rest of the story-telling drivellers."

"But you know I do! And don't talk about your father's correspondences,—I hate them too."

"Well, what *shall* we talk of?" said George, plucking a little heathbell out from the grass at the top of the cliff, and holding it contemplatively and smiling. "Now look at this!

'There's not a flower of spring'"—

"Stop there," said Edith; "for this is nearing autumn, and if you talk of the flowers, be accurate."

"Well, I was going to say," George continued, "in the words of Mrs. Browning, that there's not a flower, whether of spring or autumn I don't care a fig, but boasts itself allied

'By significance
And correspondence to that spirit world,
Outside the limits of our space and time,
Whereto we are bound.'

There are poetry and correspondences both together. Why don't you run away?"

"Now don't be stingy, George. Let us talk about something else; about"—

"Love!" said George,—"everlasting love!"

"No," said Edith, "because that is sheer nonsense. There may be love for a day, or for a year, but love for ever is impossible."

"Why?"

"Because," said Edith, "the Church only fixes it till death us do part, and that is not for ever, is it?"

"Oh! but that is not Scripture," said George.

"A deal you know about Scripture!" said Edith. "Are we not told there is to be no love in the resurrection?"

"No love?" said George; "no love, no life!"

"No love,—only of God," said Edith; "for in the resurrection we shall be as the angels."

"And don't *they* love?"

"Why, yes," said Edith, blushing; "but only as men love men, and women love women!"

"Dear me!" said George. "Then angels love very genteelly and very coolly, not with throbbing hearts and leaping pulses, and when we rise we shall leave the best part of our life behind us! The love of the youth that only breaks into leaf and blossom in the presence of a maiden, and the love of the maiden that shrinks into shade except in the presence of the youth, all dead and withered, and nothing left but what is very calm and respectable?"

"How should it be otherwise?" said Edith.

"I think it is otherwise," said George; "or life is a mockery. I cannot think that God has drawn our souls together only to sever them."

"Ah, George, that's all sentiment," said Edith; "you know in heaven they neither marry nor are given in marriage. That is quite plain; and whatever our wishes may be, it is no use to think we shall ever indulge them."

"I don't believe God allows us to have orderly and proper wishes without providing that they shall be indulged. Everything has its wish. The crocodile

by its nature wishes for the water, and there it is.
The tiger wishes for the lamb and the jungle, and there
they are.   What God does for crocodiles and tigers
surely He does for men and women.   If we wish for
everlasting love, surely He gives it us."

"We may wish for it while we are in this world, but
when we go into the next our nature may be wholly
changed, and we may not wish for it there."

"Why, we are made up of loves, or desires, or wishes,"
said George; "and if they be changed by our removal
from this world, we ourselves shall be changed.   If our
desires lose all identity with those we now possess, and
be changed into something else, we shall also lose our
identity and be in like manner changed.   Surely your
affections and wishes will be those proper to a woman,
and mine will be those proper to a man."

"But you know it is said, 'In heaven they neither
marry nor are given in marriage.'"

"Well, if you and I marry it will be on earth, and
then you know we shall not need to marry in heaven, if
we attain to the resurrection of the just."

"Oh! that is a mere quibble, George."

"Certainly not, Edith.   In heaven all are as the angels
of God, that is, *paired souls*.   That is what Jesus meant
when He said, 'They neither marry nor are given in
marriage; but are as the angels of God.'   Every man is
by virtue of his entrance into heaven a husband, and
every woman by virtue of her entrance a wife.   They
are those whom God has joined together, and who are
not to be put asunder."

"Well, I never heard the thing put in that way
before.   I always thought when Jesus said, 'But are

as the angels of God,' He meant that all are single in heaven."

"Nothing in this world is single, Edith, and certainly nothing is single in the spiritual world. Why did Jesus attach so much importance to marriage, and why is the infringement of its sanctities made all through the Scriptures so heinous a sin? Not for temporal reasons only. Jesus said, 'Wherefore they are *no more* twain, but one flesh.' Never again twain; consequently for ever one."

"I certainly never thought of it so," said Edith; "but there is some reason in what you say."

"Consider. If married partners are made one on earth, of course they neither marry nor are given in marriage in heaven, for the spiritual conjunction has already been effected."

"That is an entirely new idea to me," said Edith; "but what about those who die as little children?"

"All little children grow up in heaven and become angels," said George.

"Then do they remain single, or are they married in heaven? That seems to me a considerable difficulty."

"It is not so great a difficulty as it looks," said George. "The little boys and girls that enter heaven are all *paired souls*. They are united by internal affinities, and when they are of mature age these affinities manifest themselves by external union. Marrying and giving in marriage, in an earthly sense, cannot exist among them; but they are together by the force of a Divine law operating upon their inmost affections."

"Then there are that large class who never marry on earth. They must either remain single, or be married in heaven?"

"Oh, here is father," said George; "he will explain it."

"The fact is," said Mr. Rivers, when the point had been placed before him, "the pure conjugal spirit is an essential element in all men and women before they enter heaven. This pure conjugal spirit can only be developed and called into exercise by one of the opposite sex. A man is not an angelic man, and consequently cannot be a candidate for heaven, unless he purely loves and is purely loved by an angelic woman. And so also in the opposite case. Thus, by the necessity of Divine law, marriages *precede* entrance into heaven."

"But I am speaking of those who die maids and bachelors," said Edith.

"And so am I," said Mr. Rivers. "You do not know that there is a world of spirits into which all such go, that they may be prepared for entrance into heaven."

"Indeed, no," said Edith; "there is nothing about it in the Scriptures, and I cannot go into that."

"But there is," said Mr. Rivers, "innumerable allusions to an intermediate state in the Scriptures."

"That is another subject," said George; "Edith and I were talking of everlasting love, which she thinks does not exist."

"What would the world be without it?" asked Mr. Rivers. "It is the veritable God! It is the veritable man! We have no other guarantee for the permanence of the universe. The sun rises to-day as it rose in ages past, and as it will rise in the inexpressibly distant future. This is because God changes not, but loves on for ever. So with man. Love is everlasting by its very nature. That passion which veers, changes, and dies, is not love."

"Certainly not," said George; "our best authors recognise this fact. For instance, Shakespeare says :

> ' Love is not love
> Which alters when it alteration finds.'

I don't know what our orthodox friends will say to that, seeing that they make God's love to alter when it alteration finds, that is, according as men believe well or ill."

"Oh, that doctrine has been long exploded," said Mr. Hawthorne, who had come up with Rivers, "and no system of religion that involves it is worth a thought. Let us get down here by this winding pathway on to the beach, and wander home by the sands, for Mrs. Rivers will be looking for us at the breakfast-table."

The friends rose, and with some little effort, which afforded a good deal of amusement, found their way down the crumbling pathway, and at length reached the beach. They had scarcely recovered breath before Hawthorne opened the subject which was now uppermost in his mind.

CHAPTER XV.

THE BREAST, WITH HEART AND LUNGS.

Hawthorne : Now we have sucked your brains, my dear Rivers, about the correspondence of the head, le us hear what you have to say about the breast.

Rivers : With its contents,—the heart and the lungs Certainly. First, with respect to its situation. It is below the head. The breast therefore corresponds with that which is inferior, and the head with that which is superior. The former corresponds with the lower love, the latter with the higher. The higher love is that of God, the lower that of the neighbour. The head corre sponds with a superior, the breast with an inferior, goodness. Hence in the vision of Daniel (ii. 31–35), the head of the great image was of gold and the breast only of silver. The former was of the superior, the latter of the inferior, metal.

Hawthorne : Then the metals are included in your scheme of correspondence?

Rivers : Yes. Gold has relation to the things of love, silver to those of wisdom. Thus, then, the Head corresponds with that goodness which is of Love, and the Breast with that goodness which is of Wisdom.

Hawthorne: What is the difference?

Rivers: Well, some people are good because they are especially loving; others are good because they are especially wise. The one class drink in their religious life from the fountain of everlasting love, the other from the fountain of everlasting wisdom. In the first class the will operates supremely, in the last the intellect.

Hawthorne: Ah, I see. The former are led by feeling, the latter by truth.

Rivers: You have hit it exactly. Thus you perceive that the Breast corresponds with the Goodness of Neighbourly Love and all that it encloses and contains.

Hawthorne: What does that goodness enclose?

Rivers: Well, a heart, and also a living respiratory force, or it would speedily contract and perish.

Hawthorne: And this prepares the way for the correspondence of the heart and the lungs?

Rivers: Yes. The Heart by virtue of its function corresponds with the Will, and the Lungs by virtue of their function correspond with the Understanding.

Hawthorne: We have had the will and understanding before as corresponding with other parts of the body.

Rivers: In the soul there are only will and understanding. They exercise various functions, and they cause the existence of bodily organs corresponding with those functions. Thus I have shown you that the ear and the eye correspond with will and understanding by virtue of their functions of hearing and seeing. I shall now show you that heart and lungs correspond with will and understanding by virtue of their functions of sustaining life in the body; the one by propelling the blood through the physical system, the other by inhaling the atmosphere to purify the blood by carrying off its corruptions.

Hawthorne : Very good.

Rivers : Well, the heart propels the blood through the entire body. You have already learned the correspondence of the blood. The blood of the soul is the living faith that feeds and nourishes the body of our charity. This faith is kept in exercise and made to flow through all the veins of the soul by the will, the loving force. Hence the heart corresponds with the will because the one does for the body what the other does for the soul. We recognise this when we speak of soft hearts and hard hearts.

Hawthorne : Those, of course, are figurative expressions?

Rivers : Yes, but founded on the great law of correspondences. A soft heart means a will easily affected, and a hard heart means a stubborn will.

Hawthorne : Undoubtedly.

Rivers : In moments of anxiety the heart aches. When the affections of our will are pained the corresponding organ in the body responds. Now because the heart corresponds with the will, we read so much about the wickedness of the heart in the Scriptures.

Hawthorne : Which I have always imputed to sheer physiological ignorance on the part of the Hebrews.

Rivers : For instance, "The heart is deceitful above all things, and desperately wicked : who shall know it?" (Jer. xvii. 9).

Hawthorne : Of course there is no wickedness in the heart of the body. It is a vital pumping engine, and so long as it does its work well it is good.

Rivers: Just so. It is the human will that is desperately wicked, and the depths of which no one can know. Thus when the Psalmist exclaims, "My heart is fixed, O God, my heart is fixed" (Ps. lvii. 7), he means that his spiritual heart, the living force of his soul, the will, is fixed on heavenly things. So God is said to search the heart; He searches the will to determine the nature of our affections. The sin of Judah is said to be "graven upon the table of their heart" (Jer. xvii. 1). Sin is impressed upon the will. A hundred instances to illustrate the correspondence of the heart might be quoted.

Hawthorne: Not only the Bible, but our familiar everyday conversation is full of it. The heart is the synonym of the affections, undoubtedly. It was so in the olden time, and it is so now.

Rivers: I may mention another passage or two by way of illustration. Jesus said, "Blessed are the pure in heart." He also said, "Out of the heart proceed evil thoughts." Neither of these phrases have any meaning unless we think of the human will. The pure in heart are those whose loves are pure. The heart that sends forth evil thoughts is the corrupt will. Then we are called upon to wash our hearts,—"O Jerusalem, wash thine heart from wickedness" (Jer. iv. 14). Ezekiel speaks of the stony heart, and the heart of flesh.

Hawthorne: That will do, my dear friend. The thing is all too obvious. But what do you say about the lungs? I have no remembrance that the lungs are anywhere mentioned in the Scriptures.

Rivers: I believe they are not; but still they have their correspondence. They correspond with the understanding. We know this from the use of the lungs. They receive into their vessels the impure blood discharged by the heart, and they serve as the purifiers of the blood, and give life to it. Not by themselves, observe ; but by means of the breath or air which they inhale. So our spirit blood—the faiths and affections circulating through our spiritual system—are purified of their grossnesses in the understanding, not by means of it, but by means of the heavenly air, the truth, which the understanding inhales.

Hawthorne : I see something of your meaning.

Rivers : Thus it is written in Psalm li. 10, "Create in me a clean heart, O God, and renew a right spirit within me." It is a clean *heart* and a right *spirit.* In the one case the organ is mentioned, in the other case its contents. Not clean *blood* and a right spirit ; nor clean heart and right *lungs.* The reason is obvious. The propulsion is of the heart, but the purification is of the air inhaled. A clean heart, of course, means a pure will. A right spirit means a correct understanding, which inhales the breath of life breathed upon us by the Saviour God for the taking away of all the impurities which heavenly faith gathers in its contact with our earthy selfish affections.

Hawthorne : But the blood is sometimes corrupted by what we breathe into the lungs.

Rivers : Certainly. If we breathe foul air, the blood forced by the heart into the lungs is tainted rather than purified. So, if we inhale the foetid airs of hell, which are falsehoods, into the understanding, the faiths and affections flowing through our souls are corrupted. What we need to breathe is the Holy Spirit, the soft airs of heaven laden with Divine odours and spiritual balms. These give vitality to our faith as pure air does to the blood. In short, my dear friend, just as the blood is purified from evil things and fed with good things from the air as it passes through the lungs, so our affections are cleansed and vitalized by the breath of truth received into our understandings. The will is the heart, and the understanding the lung, of the soul.

Hawthorne : As a mere figure of speech I can receive all this readily. But you will not endeavour to make me believe that after death spirits have hearts and lungs?

Rivers : I shall insist upon it.

Edith : Dear me, Mr. Rivers, this is carrying the thing · all too far.

Rivers : Why so, Edith?

Edith : Well, because it is so silly.

George : We shall be strange beings surely, Edith, if we have no hearts! We are to love God with all our hearts, and do you think we shall have no hearts to love Him with?

Rivers : Men and women in the spiritual world are real substances, not simply shadows. They are not hollow forms. They have hands for their harps, and heads for their crowns. So I think we must allow that they have hearts for their loves, and lungs to breathe the heavenly aromas.

Edith : It is really so absurd to think of spirits having lungs!

George : How do you think the angels could blow their trumpets without them?

Edith : You always have some ridiculous suggestion to make.

Rivers: I could tell you of a man who spoke to the angels, and they told him that they could feel the pulsation of the heart in the chest, and of the artery at the wrist, like men in the natural world.

Edith: Well, that I never *will* believe, Mr. Rivers.

Rivers: Elias and Moses were seen on the Mount. Men were seen at the sepulchre in shining garments. Do you think their humanity consisted of empty shapes, and that there was nothing inside them?

Edith: It is a subject on which I will not argue, but I know it is not true.

Hawthorne: That is the sublime of unreason, my dear. It is difficult for me to realize all that Mr. Rivers tells me of the life after death, and of the men and women in the spiritual world. I can only say, that if it is all a dream, I regret it, and I wish the vision were a reality.

Rivers: I am afraid that the great bulk of Christians think of spirits as mere animated *forms*. But have they considered that form is only a condition of substance? Without substances there would be no forms. Then they think of spirits as mere shadows with forms. But have they considered that there can be no shadows without substances? If men have forms and shadows in another life, they must be substances. If substances, they are not hollow like drums; but in every way full and perfect as men on earth, having hearts, lungs, and an interior organization adapted to the world in which they live. Their hearts are their wills, which send their affections flowing and circulating like blood through every part of their spiritual system, and their lungs are their understandings, into which the purifying breath of heaven is inhaled to cleanse and give vital force to those affections when they get dulled and clogged with the humours contracted in our selfish and worldly natures. But there is ma' beckoning to us from the window, and getting impatient.

CHAPTER XVI.

THE SHOULDER, ARM, HAND, FINGERS, THUMB.

Hawthorne: I think, Rivers, the image described in Daniel to which you have before referred had its arms of silver as well as its breast. Was that from correspondence?

Rivers: Undoubtedly. The head of gold because it has relation to love, the breast and arms of silver because it has relation to truth.

Hawthorne: Well, what is the correspondence of the arm?

Rivers: The arm is made up of several parts. There is the shoulder. Its use is to push and to bear. There is the arm proper. Its use is for work, and, if needful, for defensive warfare. There is the hand, composed of palm, fingers, and thumb. Its use is to grasp. Now in these is concentrated the power of the body. An armless man is useless. The Arm, therefore, in all its parts corresponds with Power. The body has its shoulder to bear, its arm to labour, and its hand to grasp and hold. So the spirit has corresponding capabilities. It has a shoulder to bear its burdens, an arm to effect its needs, a hand to grasp and hold its facts. But that is only one view of the subject. The fingers, hand, arm, and shoulder have multifarious uses, and according to these they correspond with the multifarious powers possessed by the soul. In this way we read in the Scriptures of the fingers, hands, and arm of the Lord. These, because of their correspondence, signify the Divine Power.

Hawthorne : You do not assert that God has such members as are ascribed to Him in the Bible?

Rivers : In relation to ourselves we must so think of Him. We can form no other conception. That is because of human incapacity. We necessarily limit Him to the highest idea of which we are capable, and that is the human idea. What God is in Himself we cannot know, because in Himself He is infinite. He is revealed to us as a man, but manhood is primarily of the soul. By the Lord's Fingers, therefore, are meant His Power of action in His universe. Thus, "When I consider Thy heavens, the work of Thy fingers, the moon and the stars which Thou hast ordained" (Ps. viii. 3). The universe is said to be the work of God's fingers because it is the effect of Divine Power.

Hawthorne : I see. But the fingers are the most insignificant parts of the arm. I wonder such fulness of power as the creation of the universe should be ascribed to them.

Rivers : I do not. Consider what a man is without fingers. He might almost as well be without an arm. The strength of the warrior is in his fingers. Thus— "Blessed be the Lord my strength, which teacheth my hands to war and my fingers to fight" (Ps. cxliv. 1). Without fingers a man could not grasp a sword or bend a bow. The sword is the truth which smites ; the bow is doctrine whence the truth is shot. The fingers therefore correspond with the power to grasp truth and direct it against our evils,—our spiritual enemies.

Hawthorne: Very good. But you have passed by the Thumb.

Rivers: The thumb is really one of the fingers as the great toe is one of the toes. But the thumb has doubtless its correspondence because of its special character as the most useful of the fingers. A man might lose one of his fingers proper and not be greatly injured; but the loss of the thumb would be irreparable. The thumb and the fingers correspond with power in all fulness, because the fulness of a man's usefulness is in the terminations of his arm. The thumb especially corresponds with such power, and hence the blood of the ram was put upon the thumb of the right hand in the consecration of Aaron and his sons. The blood of the ram is truth from goodness, and man is consecrated to the service of God by truth touching the extremest power of his soul. We read in Judges i. 6, that Judah, having overcome Adonibezek, cut off his thumbs and his great toes. This represents the deprivation of power. Our evils being overcome, we deprive them of ability again to hurt us.

Hawthorne: A barbarous proceeding surely! Was this cruelty done to exhibit the beauty of correspondences?

Rivers: Certainly not! The age was a barbarous one. The people were hard and cruel. Their cruelties could not be restrained, but only directed and guided. The acts done in cruelty correspond as well as those done in mercy. Then we read of God's Hand and of

His right Hand, the former corresponding with His power
by truth, the other with His power by goodness. Thus
it is said, "His hand shall *lead* me and His right hand
shall *hold* me." We are *led* by truth, but *sustained* by
goodness. The right hand of God also corresponds
with omnipotence. Hence Jesus is said to be at the
right hand of God, that is to say, He is in possession of
all power. So we are told to cut off the offending right
hand. We are not to mutilate our bodies, which could
serve no useful purpose, and might terminate in death,
thus involving suicide. We are to dissever from ourselves offensive powers. The offending right hand is
power from evil. This should be alienated from the
soul. I might give you a hundred illustrations of the
correspondence of the hands. For instance, there is the
lifting up of the hands, which signifies the elevation of
our powers. There are the bloody hand and the clean
hand. The one is the power devoted to evil, the other
to good.

Hawthorne : It is too late for me to dispute either
your arguments or your illustrations.

Rivers : So, mention is made of the Arm of God. The
everlasting arm is the power of God to upbear the soul
for ever. God is said to make bare His holy arm. His
own arm is said to bring salvation to Him. It is written
(Ps. xcviii. 1), "His right hand and holy arm hath
gotten Him the victory." The baring of His arm signifies
the revelation of His power. The right hand and holy
arm that get the victory mean the power of goodness and
truth that triumphs over evil !

Hawthorne : Yes, that too is sufficiently obvious.

Rivers : Again, the arm of the wicked is said to be

broken, which of course means that the power of the evil for mischief is overruled. But we might go on to any length with these illustrations.

Hawthorne: Doubtless. You have said nothing about the Palms.

Rivers : These also have their correspondence. Anything grasped in the palm of the hand is in the person's own proper possession. The palm therefore corresponds with one's own proper power. Whatever is in the palm is at the person's disposal, and thus the palm corresponds with what is peculiarly the grasping and retaining power of the spirit.

George: Beautifully presented to us by Browning, and suggestive in every point :

> " Only, for man, how bitter not to grave
> On his *soul's hands' palms* one fair good wise thing
> Just as he grasped it ! "

The soul has its power of grasping goodness and wisdom, and this power is its palm.

Edith: Oh, that's borrowed! Give us something original.

George: Borrowed ? Where is it borrowed from, Edith ?

Edith: There is something like it in the Bible.

Rivers: Edith is thinking of Isa. xlix. 16 : " Behold, I have graven thee upon the palms of my hands." This passage the more fully illustrates our subject. It refers to the Church which God has in His own proper possession. The spirit's palm is its power to hold.

Hawthorne: Neither can I object to that view.

Edith : Why, pa', you are getting quite a convert to this strange theology.

Hawthorne: Not so, my dear. I must admit what

is reasonable. The whole thing, however, has to be reviewed. All this about the hand and arm might, I believe, be illustrated from the writings of men of genius. It enters into our ordinary conversation. When we say a man's hands are not clean, we understand what is meant. So, when we say a man has an itching palm, or greedy fingers, or a long arm, or broad shoulders, we naturally interpret the phrases as having relation to his mental peculiarities. The Bible may be constructed, as I have before said, on some natural law of symbols.

George: Which natural law is, as it seems to me, that of correspondences.

Edith: But are we, when we read the Bible, to be always reasoning with ourselves and looking into a dictionary of correspondences before we can know what is meant?

Rivers: That is not the way to read the Bible, Edith. We are to read it in an intelligent and reverential spirit, when light will stream from it into our understandings. We are not to read it as we spell our way through a book written in a language which we only half understand. When you walk into a garden there are thousands of beauties around you, but you might pause at every simple flower, and stand discussing and investigating its wonderful structure and meanings half the day, and so lose the charm and loveliness of the whole. To read the Bible is one thing; to investigate and explore its secrets is another. We should do both.

Hawthorne: We have yet to consider the correspondence of the Shoulder.

Rivers: As I have said, the shoulder corresponds with power in its highest degree. This may be illustrated by what Isaiah (ix. 6) prophesied of Jesus, that "the government shall be upon His shoulder." The government of the whole universe of spirit and nature rests upon God. The shoulder which sustains the weight of that responsibility is the Divine Omnipotence. The Divine Humanity of Jesus is the shoulder of the Eternal. Thus He said, "*All power* is given unto me in heaven and in earth." Hence, as we read in Isa. xxii. 22, it is prophetically said of Jesus that "the key of the house of David" should be laid upon His shoulder. The possession of a key is significative of power, because he who has the key of a place has power over it; and this key is said to be upon the shoulder of Jesus, because His Humanity upbears all things. Again, it is prophetically said of the tribe of Benjamin (Deut. xxxiii. 12), "And the Lord shall cover him all the day long, and he shall dwell between His shoulders." What is meant there obviously is security in the Divine Power. So, in the parable, the lost sheep when found is laid on the shoulders rejoicing.

Edith : Of course, that is a very natural way of carrying a sheep. You cannot wish to make out that anything else is meant by that?

Rivers : Why, yes. The statement is connected with a parable, and everything in a parable has a special meaning. The recovered sheep is the goodness acquired by repentance, and which is in consequence made secure and held by man's highest capabilities. The goodness that has never been lost or tried is not half so much ours as the goodness first missed and then won by toil and pain. That once recovered is safe on our spiritual shoulders.

Hawthorne: Ah, your argument amounts to this, that the entire *limb* from the shoulder to the fingers corresponds with *power* in some of its phases.

Rivers: Yes, including the elbows, wrists, and joints of the fingers and thumb. It must be so. Soul is cause, body is effect. Force is primarily in the soul and by derivation in the body. The latter is moulded after the fashion of the former. If there were no spiritual arm there would be no natural arm. Spirit puts forth its counterpart in nature; the substance necessarily casts a corresponding shadow. The arm of the angel that it may work in nature must clothe itself with an arm of flesh. An armless angel could no more do the work required of him in heaven than an armless man could do the work required of him on earth.

Edith: Why don't you quote us something else, George? You might give us that well-worn thing about Divine philosophy, which is not harsh and crabbed,—and —what else?

George: Why, Edith, like your conversation when you are in your best moods—

> " A perpetual feast of nectar'd sweets,
> Where no crude surfeit reigns."

INTERLUDE X.

"THE SPIRITS IN PRISON."

DURING the evening Mr. Hawthorne took the opportunity to refer to what Mr. Rivers had said about an Intermediate State.

"I have always," he said, "regarded this as a superstition of the Roman Catholics, invented by the priests to raise money."

"The Roman Catholic idea of purgatory has in it the rudiments of a truth," said Rivers.

"You surprise me," said Hawthorne; "it is generally held by those Christians who are not Roman Catholic that the departed soul goes to heaven or hell."

"Of course," said Edith; "that at least is taught very plainly in the Bible."

"Where, my dear?" asked Mr. Rivers.

"Why, in the parable of the sheep and the goats. Were not the sheep at once taken to heaven, and were not the goats told at once to depart to hell?"

"But where were the sheep and the goats when they were judged?"

"Where? why, in—in—heaven, I suppose."

"What, the goats admitted into heaven! The evil received into the kingdom of God!"

"Yes, certainly, for does it not say, 'Depart, ye cursed'?"

"It does; but I want to know *whence* they were to depart. It appears to me that both the sheep and the goats had to go elsewhither; for it says, 'And these shall go away into everlasting punishment; but the righteous into life eternal.' The righteous had to go into life eternal and the wicked into death eternal."

"Well, if you put it in that way," said Edith, "I don't know what we are to believe."

"We are to believe that there is an Intermediate State which is not 'everlasting punishment' nor 'life eternal.' In this Intermediate State all are after they depart out of this world. This is the scene of judgment. It is a monstrous supposition that the evil are accepted in heaven to be judged, and after having been admitted are cast out. The sheep and the goats are mixed together in the Intermediate State, and God there separates them, the one rising into heaven the other descending into hell."

"This is altogether a new view, Mr. Rivers," said Edith. "And do you want us to discard all the things we have been taught?"

"I want you to discard such things as are not true," said Mr. Rivers. "The scene of the parable of the sheep and the goats is the same as the scene in which John saw all the wonderful things described in the book of Revelation."

"Which I say was nothing but a dream," said Edith.

"*He* does not say it was a dream," said Mr. Rivers; "but, on the contrary, he says, 'I was in the Spirit,'—that is to say, in a spiritual state,—or, in other words, the spiritual world. Every one in the Spirit has his senses opened into the spiritual world."

"Then I should say that John was in the third heaven, where Paul went and saw and heard things ineffable," said Edith.

"I should say he was not," said Mr. Rivers, "and I will tell you why. He could not be in heaven, because he saw angels come down from heaven above him; and he could not be in hell, because he saw the devil cast into the bottomless pit beneath him."

"Very good," said Mr. Hawthorne, smiling at his daughter's evident discomfiture; "you must confess yourself beaten there, Edith."

"Thus, for instance," continued Rivers, "in the 20th chapter John says, 'I saw an angel *come down* from heaven,' and he goes on to say that he saw the angel take hold of the dragon and 'cast him *into the bottomless pit.*' It is quite obvious that John was in an Intermediate State. He was not where the angel came from, and he was not where the dragon was cast."

"There, that will do for you, Edith," said Mr. Hawthorne; "it is quite evident that your teachers have not instructed you in the profoundest theology. But, Rivers, what is your philosophy of all this?"

"Why this," said Mr. Rivers; "men when they die are neither good enough for heaven nor evil enough for hell. Consider, heaven is pure goodness and truth. No one when he leaves this world is in a state of perfect purity. Hell is nothing but evil and falsehood. None are wholly evil. Therefore as a necessary consequence men at first are neither in the one nor the other. Higher and purer truths in the world of spirits purify the good, and drive the evil into their very lusts, thus exalt the one class to heaven, and hurl the other to hell."

" What, Truth hurl to hell ! You amaze me."

" Certainly.   Truth is the sifting and separating force. Truth shines with a full clear light in the world of spirits, and the good follow it as it grows brighter and brighter and its guidance terminates in heaven. On the other hand, the evil hate the light and turn and flee from it, and it pursues them till they find themselves in the darkness of hell, where they get rest from its searching rays."

" Ah, the same force draws the one to heaven and drives the other to hell ? "

" Yes.   That is how it is put before us by the Lord. ' He that doeth truth cometh to the light ;' ' Every one that doeth evil hateth the light.'   The light tests and separates."

" But that is spoken about people in this world," said Edith.

" It is spoken about the operation of light or truth upon the human mind. It is the same whether men be in the natural world or the spiritual world. Truth draws the good and repels the evil always and everywhere."

" Man is man whatever world he be in," said George ; "he is not changed in his nature by the simple act of removal."

"No," said Mr. Rivers. "Moreover, it was concerning men in the world of spirits, or in the Intermediate State, that Peter wrote when he said that Jesus 'went and preached unto the spirits in prison.' The spirits in prison were those who were in the Intermediate State."

" What authority have you for that?" asked Hawthorne.

"Well, that those spirits were not in heaven is clear from the context, because it is said they were aforetime disobedient, and also from the fact that the place where they were is called a prison. That they were not in hell is clear from the fact that Christ went to preach to them, with, of course, a view to their removal. They were evidently not in their final state, but in one out of which they might be lifted by instruction."

"You think spirits cannot be lifted out of hell?"

"No. They lack the will : evil is their goodness. They lack the intellectual perceptive power : falsehood is their truth. Thus, when the thing that saves is shown to the devils, they regard it as an enemy. The good they take to be evil and the truth they take to be falsehood. They abhor the warmth and light of heaven and flee from them. Their natures are perverted, and they see everything upside down. The Intermediate State is a prison in which the good and the evil are locked until some force comes to liberate them. The Intermediate State is a prison to the good because their heavenly love has not free play, and it is a prison to the evil because their lusts, which can only have full exercise in hell, are restrained. Now the key that unlocks the gates of the Intermediate State is Truth. As I have hinted, Truth opens heaven and draws the good thither, and it opens hell and drives the evil into its portals. Christ went and preached to the spirits in prison. In other words, He took to them the Truth. This truth was the liberating force. It was the light to which the good came and found their heaven, and from which the evil fled and found their hell."

"Ah," said Hawthorne, "I perceive there is a whole world of philosophy in your religion, and that it requires thought and study to master it. I am sorry I did not look into it before. I am quite unprepared to combat it. I may confess this—I never thought to find that so much could be said for doctrines which I have considered so objectionable, and which appeared to be the outgrowth of barbarism and superstition."

"Not to be accepted by any sane man?" asked George.

"Truly," said Hawthorne, "that was exactly what I did think."

"So thought the pagan sages when Christianity first arose," replied George. "But the simple Love in the breasts of the simple martyrs mastered and has outgrown the lordly Intelligences of the ancients. Their philosophies and theosophies have faded and fallen before the one precept of the One Man, 'Love one another.' Can you understand it?"

"I cannot," said Hawthorne, thoughtfully stroking his beard and rising from his chair, thus for the present terminating the discussion.

In consequence of various engagements and occupations, an opportunity for renewing the subject of correspondences did not occur till the day before the little party were to return home, when Hawthorne in a quiet moment again brought it before the notice of Mr. Rivers.

CHAPTER XVII.

THE LEG, FOOT, TOES.

Hawthorne: I think, Rivers, to complete your series of correspondences you have to tell us something of the legs and their analogue in the soul.

Rivers: The Legs and the Feet. Their correspondence may be known by their position and use. First, with respect to their use. They are for progression. By means of the legs and feet we move from one *place* to another. They therefore correspond with those spiritual faculties by the exercise of which we move from one *state* to another. We move onward or backward as we do good or evil. We are nearing heaven as we obey the Divine commandment, "*Walk* before me and be thou perfect" (Gen. xvii. 1); or we are nearing hell as we *walk* in the counsel of the ungodly (Ps. i. 1). We may go forward or backward, or be lame and have to stand still. Some men have a kind of paralysis in their spiritual legs and make no progress. This may arise from want of will or want of understanding, or both. The right leg or the left leg, or both, may be inoperative. The Lord's curing the halt and the lame has a spiritual significance. An influx of Divine life into the will and understanding is needed to effect motion in the soul and help its journey heavenward.

Hawthorne : Are we not told that God "taketh not pleasure in the legs of a man"? (Ps. cxlvii. 10).

Rivers : That should show you that the legs have a spiritual signification.   It would be a mere absurdity to say that God has no pleasure in the muscle and bone that make up the natural legs.   Man's self-derived power of action—those faculties which he exercises in the pushing forward in his own way, in progressing in science and life under the guidance of Sense rather than Revelation —is not in accordance with the Divine pleasure.

Hawthorne : Man's progress in science—whether by the use of what you call his self-derived powers or otherwise—is not to be despised.

Rivers : Such progress ends in the quagmires in which hundreds of powerful minds have stuck fast.   Agnosticism is a swamp in which such progress terminates.   The legs of a great number of men of late years have run into that slough of despond, that "gospel of dirt," named "Denial of Revelation."   In these God can have no pleasure.

Hawthorne : I perceive your meaning without admitting the perfect accuracy of your indictment against the scientists.

Rivers : Then you may see the correspondence of the legs and feet from their position.   They are the *lowest* parts of the body.   Hence they correspond with the lowest things of the soul.   They relate to those things in the spirit which are just above our merely material nature, and which rest upon it as the foot does upon the earth. You may see this in relation to what is said about the image to which we have already referred. The head was of gold, the breast of silver, the legs of iron and clay. The head has relation to the highest states of the soul, love ; the breast to those immediately beneath, wisdom ; and the legs to those below all, mere action. In other words, the head corresponds with celestial, the breast with spiritual, and the legs with natural states.

Hawthorne : Definitions which I don't a bit understand.

Rivers : We must have words to express things. I suppose you will admit that there are higher and lower conditions of the mind, and that the higher conditions rest upon the lower as their foundation ?

Hawthorne : I cannot object to that.

Rivers : Our lowest state is our natural state, that into which we are born. We grow upward into a spiritual state, and this we have attained to when we know there is a God and we have faith in Him as our Father. Then, you know, faith may aspire upward, and out of it may grow a state of love, which we call celestial. Our religious life is then like a perfect man. The head rests upon the breast, and the breast on the legs and feet. The celestial is supported by the spiritual, and the spiritual by the natural. Love stands upon Faith, and faith on Action.

Hawthorne : The arrangement is orderly.

Rivers : Now what, from the literalist's point of view, can be meant by God's feet and His footstool ? His feet are of course the Divine in its lowest manifestation. By the Feet of God are meant His Humanity, because it is by virtue of His Humanity that He has a standing in the Church. In this sense the Church is His footstool.

M

Thus, "Heaven is My throne, and the earth is My footstool; where is the house that ye build unto me? and where is the place of My rest?" (Isa. lxvi. 1). It is perfectly obvious that, as the throne signifies the Church in heaven where the Divine King reigns, the footstool signifies the Church on earth where the humanity of the Divine King is seen. So again, "We will go into His tabernacles; we will worship at His footstool." No one can mistake the meaning of such utterances as these.

Hawthorne: They are evidently poetic and figurative.

Rivers: Of course you remember the exclamation, "How beautiful upon the mountains are the feet of Him that bringeth good tidings." The feet there signify the Divine Humanity touching with heavenly beauty the lofty principles of charity and faith in the Church. Well, whenever we read about the feet of God in the Scriptures, we are to understand the Divine in lowest things—in the natural mind—in man as he is in nature. In relation to man, the Foot signifies the Natural Mind itself, because on that the higher spiritual states rest.

Hawthorne: When it says somewhere in the Pentateuch that the foot of the Israelites did not swell in the wilderness, does it mean that their natural minds did not swell?

Rivers: It means that their ability to go forward on their journey was never taken from them. The faculty of progression always remains healthy with the Christian. His spiritual states of perception, and his natural states of action, which include his powers of walking in the path of duty, are always kept in normal exercise. The circumstance recorded in Deuteronomy viii. 4, that the foot of the Israelites did not swell during all the forty

years they were in the wilderness, is significative of
Christian experience grounded in correspondence. During all the trials and troubles—the wilderness condition—
of the godly man, he is ever going forward—never
pausing from incapacity of action. He is sustained
so that his foot does not swell. He is held up so that
he does not dash his foot against a stone (Ps. xci. 12).
When his foot slippeth the mercy of God sustains him
(Ps. xciv. 18). When the lion and the adder, the
young lion and the dragon, are in his pathway, he tramples
them under his feet (Ps. xci. 13).

Hawthorne : Yes. All those references are very good
illustrations of your point.

Rivers : It is the lowest part of our spiritual man—
what we call the Natural Mind—that is in danger of
swelling, and therefore faltering in the hour of trial. It
is the natural mind that is liable to come into contact
with and be injured by the hard stones of falsehood. It
is the natural mind that has the propensity to slip. It is
the natural mind that the adder and the lion of passion
may assail. It is the natural mind, therefore, that God in
all the passages referred to is represented as preserving.

Hawthorne : And I suppose that is how you explain
the command of Jesus that we should wash one another's
feet?

Rivers : A very important suggestion. Jesus washed
Peter's feet, and said, " If I wash thee not thou hast no
part with me." Nobody can suppose that a part with
Jesus is to be obtained by washing the natural feet with
natural water.

Hawthorne : Of course not.

Rivers : Well, Peter saw there was some significance

in it, and asked to have his whole body washed; but Jesus said, "He that is washed needeth not save to wash his feet." In this statement He indicated that what requires cleansing is the natural mind; that to the natural mind all defilements cling; and that to this mind the water of Divine truth needs to be applied. The Lord washed the feet of His disciples to show that He cleanses the spiritual feet of the universal discipleship from the defilements they contract through their intimate commerce with the world.

Hawthorne: But then what are we to understand by the command to cut off the offending foot and cast it from us? Can we cut off the offending natural mind and get rid of it? This seems to me to involve you in some difficulty.

Rivers: Not at all. You think of the foot spiritually and of the act of cutting off and casting away literally! Thus *you* make the difficulty. The offending foot is the natural mind—the faculty of action—engaged in offensive works. To cut it off is to dissever this faculty in its offensive relationships from all Affection, and to cast it away is to remove it from all Thought. The offending foot is evil in operation, and this being perceived, we should cut it off from our wills and cast it out from our understandings. Have you yet a difficulty?

Hawthorne: Yes, because it says, "It is better for thee to enter halt into life, than having two feet to be cast into hell."

Rivers: My dear friend, all who enter into life must do so halt. None can enter into life with the full confidence that they are strong and able to walk capably in the path of righteousness. Man must confess his deficiency.

He must see his weakness,—that at best he can only stumble along like a lame man. That furnishes God with the opportunity to admit him into life. Those who have confidence in their own powers—in the soundness of their two feet—are necessarily lost. They want no help, and decline to receive it. It is a picture of mental states, and as such it is perfect.

Hawthorne: I cannot sufficiently thank you for your suggestive remarks. They deserve to be well thought over. They are, however, so new to me that I cannot so thoroughly appreciate them as you would wish. Occasionally your interpretations and definitions seem fantastic, and, if you don't mind it, I may say absurd. Still, as I have acknowledged, most of them are suggestive and demand investigation.

Rivers: That is all that I can ask for them. The Heel and the Sole have both similar correspondences. They have relation to the lower and baser powers of the soul. The serpent was to bruise the heel of the woman's seed. The serpent is the sensual force which attacks and injures the lower or carnal nature. It was said of the disobedient Jews that from " the sole of the foot even to the head there is no soundness." This, of course, signifies that they were corrupt from the highest to the lowest things of the spirit. One of the direst curses uttered by Moses (Deut. xxviii. 35) against the Israelites in case they were disobedient was this : " The Lord shall smite thee in the knees, and in the legs, with a sore blotch that cannot be healed, from the sole of thy foot unto the top of thy head." Do you see its significance ?

Hawthorne: It seems to favour your idea of the whole body being the correspondence of the soul ; and that as the soul of the evil man becomes infected with disease, so does the body.

Rivers: I perceive that at least you have obtained a general view of the subject of our discussion. The body and the soul are two as one. There could be no body without a soul, and no soul without a body.

Hawthorne: What?

Rivers: The soul must have a material or a substantial body; in other words, a natural or a spiritual body. There is the strictest correspondence between them. Here there is more or less of a correspondence between their states; so that, generally speaking, a healthy soul will inhabit a healthy body, and *vice versâ*. Because of this the curse was uttered. When the whole soul became one great blotch, it was told the Jews that their bodies should be so. In consequence of our mixed condition in the natural world, receiving healthful influences from heaven and baleful from hell, states are not now fully represented in the body. In the spiritual world they will be. A deformed soul will, as I have before hinted, make for itself a deformed body. Where the interior is diseased there will be a diseased exterior. There will work what you have called the Nemesis of existence. But, on the other hand, this involves a perfect reward for the righteous in the spiritual world. A loving Will means there a sound Heart; a wise Understanding means there active Lungs; and these will send life and vigour and beauty throughout the whole spiritual constitution.

CONCLUSION.

THE DEPARTURE.

THE last day of the stay of the little party at the seaside had come. The morning dawned bleak and thunderous, and they could not spend their time in the open air. They could only stand at the window and watch the driving rain and the stormy billows. There was in the scene a fascination which compensated them for the loss of exercise. The lowering clouds over the ocean, with the tossing waves and the labouring vessels sometimes half lost in the swelling waters, formed a grand picture from which the three gentlemen could not withdraw their eyes.

"Who can witness such force and not believe in God?" said George.

"Who can witness it and not doubt it?" asked Hawthorne, who had got back into his sceptical mood.

"What! doubt Force when you see it in operation?"

"I don't doubt Force, George," said Hawthorne, "but what you call God."

"Can you see Force and not believe in Him who wields it?"

"Oh, Force exists in Nature; there is no necessity to go beyond that."

"Why, my dear friend," said Rivers, "Nature is evidently the product, not the producer, of force. Can a thing be at once the active and the passive, the cause and the effect? Suppose I were to take you into a room filled with machinery working at full speed. You would see an exhibition of force. Would you stand before the revolving wheels and the moving levers, and say, 'Here is force; it exists *in* the machinery, and there is no necessity to go beyond it'? Would you not say, 'How is all this force put into operation? What is its origin? What turns the wheels and moves the levers? The force cannot originate in the machines themselves.'"

"I certainly should not say that the force was *in* the machinery itself," said Hawthorne, "because I know that machines are worked by forces outside of themselves, and I should thence conclude that it was so with the particular instance you brought under my notice."

"You would come to this conclusion from the necessity of the thing, your experience and instruction proving that necessity. You would know that the moved requires a mover."

"How is it in the case of a man? He moves himself."

"Oh no; the man moves his body. When you lift your arm there is an active and passive. The mover is the man—the will; the thing moved is the arm. As with one member, so with the whole body. Nature is to the Supreme will what your body is to your will. But allow me to continue my illustration. You see the machinery working in the machine-room, and you conclude that something moves the pulleys and keeps the thing in motion. An uninstructed savage would not think so. He would think, as he did of the watch, that the machinery was alive and moved of itself. You are in precisely his position when you look on Nature and say that its force is in itself. But I might take you out of the machine-room into the engine-room, and here you would be nearer the origin of force, but still not at its source. You would know that the engine did not move of itself, but that it had a mover. In pushing your investigations further back you would get at the knowledge of the steam operating to move the engine. Now the steam is not visible in the machine-room. The machines give no hint of it. It is not visible even in the engine-room. Both machine and engine are silent on the cause of their motion to the unenlightened mind of the barbarian. You push back your inquiry beyond the steam to the fire, and from the fire to the man who kindled it in the furnace and supplied it with fuel. Thus you learn that the whole thing is moved by Mind or Spiritual Force, which is invisible. You *see* operations in every stage, but not the force that produced them all. So with Nature. You are standing here in the machine-room. You don't even see the engine, much less have you penetrated to the hidden spirit fires and the Divine Man who keeps them burning."

"Well, but look at the ruthless character of the force," said Hawthorne. "How many lives have been lost in the whelming waves within the scope of our own vision! If there be a force behind nature, it must be a blind, merciless force, having no regard to human distress."

"That is another of the shallow conclusions of 'philosophy,'" said Mr. Rivers. "We have seen that there is a force behind nature moving it to results as man moves the machinery. Now this force must inhere in a subject. That subject must be a person."

"Why must it be a person?" asked Hawthorne.

"Well, then, I will say that that subject must be a 'something.' Now that something must be intelligent, because the force is directed to intelligent issues. The sun that gives the seasons, the earth that gives her fruits, sufficiently prove that point. But this intelligent something must not be called a person. What shall we call it?"

"We associate with the idea of person the human form," said Hawthorne; "and, though you have stated it several times during our conversations, I cannot think of God in that way."

"Now, Mr. Hawthorne," said George, "in one day you have gone the whole way back from the point toward which father has been leading you,—the acknowledgment of God as man, since man, of whom we have been speaking, is in the image of God. In every case concerning the body it has been shown that there are corresponding things in the human soul and in the Divine Being."

"Mr. Hawthorne cannot think of the Intelligent Something as a person," said Mr. Rivers, "because the idea of 'person' is associated with the idea of 'man.' Now the Intelligent Something must be associated with some form. Suppose we imagine it to be that of an animal?"

"Ridiculous!" said Hawthorne.

"Then we must come to the human idea, after all," said Rivers.

"The idea adopted by the highest thinkers of the age," said George. "It is repeated over and over again by that most thoughtful of all England's poets, Robert Browning. He says, in the Epistle of the old Arab physician to his master Abib, respecting what he had heard of Jesus from Lazarus, who was raised from the dead—

> 'The very God! think, Abib, dost thou think?
> So the All-Great were the All-Loving too ;—
> So through the thunder comes a *human* voice,
> Saying, "O heart I made, a heart beats here !
> Face, my hands fashioned, see it in myself.' "

A human voice—a human heart—and a human face, of which ours is but the reflection."

"Well, then, despite my friend Hawthorne's objection, we will assume that the Intelligent Something is a Divine Man. Besides, is not Intelligence itself Human? At any rate, intelligence is nothing else, for it is not mineral, vegetable, nor bestial. Now, my friend says that this Divine Man uses His force ruthlessly. He not only gives us sun, moon, and stars, with the sweet fruits and fair flowers of the earth, but also tossing waves, and when men go amongst them He allows the waves to drown them. Hawthorne would prefer that this Divine Person who exercises force in Nature should stop that force when men are in danger."

"What good would that work?" said George.

"You may well ask that," said his father. "Suppose the manager of the machines of which we have been speaking, instead of teaching his boys by their own intelligence to guard against danger, taught them to believe that, however great their follies and wilfulnesses, no machine would ever hurt them, because it would be stopped the moment they were in peril! What sort of boys would such grow to be? They would be children all their lives, and never develope into manhood. We have to be disciplined into manhood, and therefore we are left to cultivate judgment and wisdom. Mr. Hawthorne asks to have God act toward us like a silly mother, who keeps her children tied to her apron-strings till she finds she has reared a lot of idiots. A wise mother sends her children abroad to learn to be men by rough experience."

"Yes," said Hawthorne, "that is true enough. I know we must be disciplined into manhood. It is, however, none the less distressful that man should be the victim of tempests, wrecks, burnings, and earthquakes."

"If your idea that there is no God and no immortality be true, then I agree with you. But "—

"What we witness here is not the play," said George; "it is only the rehearsal, and we are being taught by a strict Master the parts we are to act hereafter, and how to play them well."

"Now," said Rivers, "a man is wrecked in the boiling surf beneath us. To our view he dies. But what happens? A strong, firm hand draws him out of the seething waters, and a kindly voice says to him, 'Were you not frightened?' 'Yes, terribly,' he says. 'Well,' says the kindly voice, 'you are all right now, are you not, and none the worse for the adventure?' 'None the worse,' is the response; 'but wiser and soberer for the experience.'"

"What do you mean?" said Hawthorne, with a look of wonderment.

"Why," said Rivers, "we in the natural world see the wrecked man die; they in the spiritual world see him introduced there safe and sound. His natural body is not drawn alive out of the waters on this side, but his spiritual body is drawn out alive on the other side. We stand on the wrong side, and only see half the incident."

"Well," said Hawthorne, walking away from the window and striding up and down the apartment, "there is no getting on with you students of Swedenborg. I think I'll become one myself."

"Do," said Mr. Rivers; "you will find your mind opened to a new world."

"And don't forget," said George, "the Victorian poets,—the Brownings, Tennyson, and Bailey,—they all run in the same line."

Mrs. Rivers and Edith at this moment entered the room. The luggage was all packed and ready, and in the next half-hour the friends were on their way to their respective homes.

The little party met again a few months afterwards, when, through the marriage of the two younger members of it, the families became more intimately united. Mr. Hawthorne had carried out his determination. He had become a student of the highest spiritual philosophy, and had lost all faith in his system of negations. In the meantime, also, the good sense of Edith had prevailed over her early prejudices, and she saw in Mr. and Mrs.

Rivers and George examples of theoretical wisdom and practical religion. People tell her that her views and those of her husband are "peculiar." She simply smiles, and says she supposes the New *is* "peculiar" when contrasted with the Old, and she is quite positive that the Old is "peculiar" when contrasted with the New.

THE END.

MORRISON AND GIBB, EDINBURGH,
PRINTERS TO HER MAJESTY'S STATIONERY OFFICE.

36 Bloomsbury Street,
London.

NEW BOOKS AND NEW EDITIONS

PUBLISHED BY

JAMES SPEIRS.

———*o*———

Amid the Corn—I. The Christmas Party. By the Author of "The Evening and the Morning." Crown 8vo, cloth, 2s.

Amid the Corn—II. The Whitsuntide Visit. By the Author of "The Evening and the Morning." Crown 8vo, cloth, 2s.

Amid the Corn—III. The Bridegroom and the Bride. By the Author of "The Evening and the Morning." Crown 8vo, cloth, 2s. *_** A Cheap Edition, in One Volume, has been issued at 4s., in cloth.

Angels (The). By a Bible Student. Second Edition. Crown 8vo, cloth, 3s. 6d.

Arbouin, James.—The Regenerate Life: Dissertations. Fcap. 8vo, cloth, 1s. 6d.

Arthur, T. S.—Beacon Lights for the Journey of Life. Fcap. 8vo, 1s. 6d.

   Anna Lee; the Maiden, Wife, and Mother. Fcap. 8vo, 2s.

Bayley, Rev. Dr.—The Divine Word Opened. Third Edition. Crown 8vo, cloth, 7s. 6d.

   Swedenborg Verified by the Progress of One Hundred Years. Crown 8vo, cloth, 2s. 6d.

   From Egypt to Canaan: The Progress of Man from the Unregenerate to the Regenerate State. Crown 8vo, cloth, 6s.

Bayley, Rev. Dr.—

The Divine Wisdom of the Word of God, as seen in the Spiritual Sense of the Histories of Samuel, Saul, David, Solomon, and Daniel. Crown 8vo, cloth, 5s.

Magnificent Scenes in the Book of Revelation. 8vo, cloth, 2s. 6d.

Scripture Paradoxes; their True Explanation. Crown 8vo, cloth, gilt edges, 2s. 6d.

Twelve Discourses on the "Essays and Reviews." 12mo, cloth, 3s.

Great Truths on Great Subjects. Six Lectures delivered at Brighton. 39th Thousand. Fcap. 8vo, cloth, gilt edges, 1s.

Christian Instruction for Young People who are of Age for Confirmation; or Dedication of themselves to a Christian Life. 18mo, sewed, 6d.; cloth, 1s.

Brayley, Ann M.—*Natural Phenomena and their Spiritual* Lessons. Crown 8vo, cloth, 3s.

Brereton, John Le Gay, M.D.—*One Teacher; One Law.* With an Appendix on the Scriptural Use of certain Anatomical Terms. Crown 8vo, sewed, 1s. 3d.

Bruce, Rev. W.—*Commentary on St. Matthew's Gospel.* Third Edition. 8vo, cloth, 7s.

Commentary on St. John's Gospel. 8vo, cloth, 7s.

Commentary on the Revelation of St. John. 8vo, cloth, 7s.

Marriage: A Divine Institution and a Spiritual and Enduring Union. 18mo, cloth, 1s. 6d.; Presentation Edition, printed in gold, and bound in white cloth, crown 8vo, 4s. 6d.

The First Three Kings of Israel. Post 8vo, cloth, 7s.

The Story of Joseph and his Brethren; its Moral and Spiritual Lessons. 18mo, cloth, 1s. 6d.

Sermons Expository and Practical. Third Edition. Fcap. 8vo, cloth, 2s. 6d.

Wesley and Swedenborg: A Review of Rev. J. Wesley's "Thoughts on the Writings of Baron Swedenborg." Crown 8vo, sewed, 3d.

Bush, Rev. Prof. George.—*Reasons for embracing the Doc*-trines and Disclosures of Emanuel Swedenborg. Fcap. 8vo, boards, 6d.

Chalklen, Rev. T.—*Sermons on the Apocalypse.* 2 Vols. crown 8vo, 5s. each.

Character ; its Elements and Development. By a Bible Student. Crown 8vo, cloth, 4s.

Circle, A, of New Church Doctrine. By the Rev. C. Giles, Rev. Dr. Bayley, Rev. S. Noble, Rev. Dr. Tafel, Rev. J. Hyde, Rev. J. Presland, Rev. W. C. Barlow, Rev. J. Ashby, Rev. J. Fox, and Hon. W. C. Howells. Fcap. 8vo, cloth, 2s.

Clowes, Rev. J.—*Illustrations of the Holy Word. Fcap. 8vo,* boards, 6d.

    The Parables of Jesus Christ Explained. Foolscap 8vo, cloth, 2s. 6d.

    Sermons (Miscellaneous), preached on Public Occasions. 8vo, cloth. Reduced from 9s. to 3s. 6d. per copy.

Clowes, Rev. John, M.A., Life and Correspondence of the. By Theodore Compton. Printed mainly in the Reformed Spelling. Crown 8vo, 1s. ; cloth, 2s. ; gilt edges, 2s. 6d.

Compendium of the Theological Works of Emanuel Sweden-borg. 8vo, cloth, 9s.

Deans, Rev. Joseph.—*A Defence of Revealed Religion ; being* Strictures upon the Views of Modern Rationalists. Fcap. 8vo, cloth, 1s. 6d.

Edleston, R.—*The Immortal Fountain ; or, Travels of Two* Sisters to the Fountain of Beauty. Seventh Edition. 18mo, cloth gilt, 1s.

Ellen French : A Tale for Girls. By Aunt Evergreen. Fcap. 8vo, cloth, 2s.

Evans, Rev. W. F.—*The Mental Cure; illustrating the Influence* of the Mind on the Body both in Health and Disease, and the Psycho-logical Method of Treatment. Fcap. 8vo, cloth, 3s.

Evening (The) and the Morning: A Narrative. Fifth Edition. Fcap. 8vo, cloth, 1s. 6d.

Field, Rev. George.—Memoirs, Incidents, and Reminiscences of the early History of the New Church in Michigan, Indiana, Illinois, and adjacent States ; and Canada. Crown 8vo, cloth, 6s.

Gateways, The, of Knowledge considered naturally and spiritually. Papers read before the Swedenborg Reading Society, Session 1880-81. Crown 8vo, sewed, 6d.

Giles, Rev. Chauncey.—Heavenly Blessedness: What it is, and how attained. In a series of Discourses on the Beatitudes. Crown 8vo, cloth, 3s.

> *The Nature of Spirit, and of Man as a Spiritual* Being. Fcap. 8vo, cloth, 1s. 6d.
>
> *Our Children in the Other Life.* Fcap. 8vo, sewed, 6d. ; cloth, 1s.
>
> *The Incarnation, Atonement, and Mediation of Jesus* Christ. Fcap. 8vo, cloth, 1s. ; boards, 6d.
>
> *The Valley of Diamonds, and other Stories for Christ-*mas and Easter. Small crown 8vo, cloth, 2s. 6d.
>
> *The Magic Shoes, and other Stories.* 18mo, *cloth,* 1s. 6d.
>
> *The Wonderful Pocket, and other Stories.* 18mo, cloth, 1s. 6d.
>
> *The Magic Spectacles: A Fairy Story.* 18mo, *cloth,* 1s. 6d.
>
> *The Gate of Pearl: A Story for Girls.* 18mo, *cloth,* 1s. 6d.
>
> *The Spiritual World and Our Children There.* Fcap. 8vo, cloth, gilt edges, 1s.

Goyder, Revs. Thomas and David G.—Spiritual Reflections for Every Day in the Year, with Morning and Evening Prayers. 3 Vols. crown 8vo, cloth, 4s. each.

Goyder, Rev. D. G.—The Heart ; its Tendency to Evil, with Hints for its Purification. With Six Plates. Sixth Edition. Crown 8vo, cloth, 2s.

> *Prayer of Prayers : considered in Five Short Lectures.* Fcap. 8vo, cloth, 1s. 6d.

Grindon, Leo H.—Figurative Language ; its Origin and Constitution. Crown 8vo, cloth, 3s. 6d.

> *Little Things of Nature considered especially in reference* to the Divine Benevolence. Crown 8vo, cloth, 2s.

Hancock, J. W., LL.B.—The Cares of the World. Crown 8vo, cloth, 3s. 6d.

Haworth, Adam.—Tract-Sermons. 18mo, cloth, 1s ; in packet, 9d.

Hayden, Rev. W. B.—Light on the Last Things. Revised and Enlarged Edition. Fcap. 8vo, cloth, 1s. 6d.

Hiller, Rev. O. Prescott.—Notes on Psalms i. to lxxvii., chiefly explanatory of their Spiritual Sense. With a New Translation from the Hebrew. 8vo, cloth, 7s.

    Posthumous Papers ; being Sermons, Short Essays, and Reflections and Maxims. Fcap. 8vo, cloth, 2s. 6d.

    Sermons on the Lord's Prayer. Fcap. 8vo, cloth, 2s.

Hindmarsh, Rev. Robert.—Rise and Progress of the New Church in England, America, and other parts. Edited by the Rev. E. Madeley. 8vo, cloth, 3s. 6d.

    The Church of England weighed in the Balance of the Sanctuary and Found Wanting ; being an examination of the Thirty-nine Articles of Religion, the three Creeds, and the Book of Common Prayer. 8vo, cloth, 3s.

    Essay on the Resurrection of the Lord ; being a humble attempt to answer the question, With what body did the Lord rise from the dead ? 8vo, 3s.

Holcombe, W. H., M.D.—Our Children in Heaven. Second Edition. Fcap. 8vo, cloth, 2s.

    The Sexes Here and Hereafter. Second Edition. Fcap. 8vo, cloth, 2s.

    The Other Life. Fcap. 8vo, cloth, 2s.

    The End of the World ; with New Interpretations of History. Fcap. 8vo, cloth, 2s. 6d.

Hughes, Lilian B.—Off the Reel: Stories. Small crown 8vo, cloth, 2s.

Hume-Rothery, Mary C.—The Wedding Guests ; or, The Happiness of Life: A Novel. Third Edition. Crown 8vo, cloth, 3s. 6d.

Hyde, Rev. John.—Emanuel Swedenborg: An Outline of His Life and Writings. Fifth Edition. Fcap. 8vo, cloth, 1s.

M'Cully (Richard).—Swedenborg Studies. Crown 8vo, cloth, 4s.

Morning Light: A New Church Weekly Journal for Years 1878, 1879, 1880, 1881, 1882, and 1883. Pp. 520, demy 4to, cloth, 8s. 6d. each.

Noble, Rev. Samuel.—Appeal on Behalf of the Doctrines of the New Church. Tenth Edition. Crown 8vo, cloth, 3s.

Noble, Rev. Samuel.—An Inquiry whether the Word in all its Integrity, though preserved, exists in any Individual Copy? Crown 8vo, sewed, 1s. ; cloth, 1s. 6d.

Our Eternal Homes. By a Bible Student. Fifth and Revised Edition. Crown 8vo, cloth, 3s.

Papers read before the Swedenborg Reading Society. Sessions 1879-80, 1880-81, 1881-82, 1882-83, 6d. each. Crown 8vo, sewed.

Parsons, Theophilus.—Deus-Homo—God-Man. Crown 8vo, cloth, 4s. 6d.

 The Infinite and the Finite. Small crown 8vo, cloth, 4s.

 Outlines of the Religion and Philosophy of Swedenborg. Small crown 8vo, cloth, 2s. 6d.

Payne, A.—A Study of the Internal or Spiritual Sense of the Fifth Book of Moses called Deuteronomy. 16mo, cloth, 2s.

Potts, Rev. J. F., B.A.—Letters from America. Crown 8vo, cloth, 3s. 6d.

Presland, Rev. John.—The Lord's Prayer: Sermons. Fcap. 8vo, cloth, 2s.

 The Creed of the New Church. Foolscap 8vo, parchment, 4s. 6d.

Proud, Rev. Joseph.—The Aged Minister's Last Legacy to the New Church. With Memoir of the Author by the Rev. E. Madeley. Crown 8vo, cloth, 2s.

 Questions of the Day. Paper before the Swedenborg Reading Society, Session 1882–83. Crown 8vo, sewed, 6d.

Richer, Edward.—The Religion of Good Sense. Third Edition. Crown 8vo, cloth, 2s. 6d.

Rodgers, Rev. R. R.—Light on Life: Essays. Post 8vo, cloth, 4s.

> *Microcosm; or, The Earth viewed as a Symbolic Record* of the History and Progressive Life of Man. Fcap. 8vo, cloth, 1s. 6d. ; limp, 1s.

Searle, Arthur H.—General Index to Swedenborg's Scripture Quotations. 8vo, cloth, 7s. 6d.

Sown in the Spring-Time: Addresses delivered to the New Church Sunday School, Camden Road. Fcap. 8vo, cloth, 1s. 6d.

Spilling, James.—Things New and Old. Small crown 8vo, cloth, 1s.

> *Our Society: A New Church without an Old Ecclesi*-asticism. Small crown 8vo, cloth, 2s. 6d.

Strutt, Elizabeth.—The Story of Psyche. Finely illustrated by John Gibson, R.A., and A. J. Strutt. Folio, cloth, gilt side and edges, 21s.

Swedenborg (Emanuel).—The Spiritual Diary, being the Record during twenty years of his Supernatural Experience. Translated by Professor G. Bush, M.A., and the Rev. J. H. Smithson. 5 Volumes. 8vo, cloth, Vols. I., II., and III., 6s. each.

Swedenborg (Emanuel).—The Brain considered Anatomically, Physiologically, and Philosophically. Edited, translated, and annotated by R. L. Tafel, A.M., Ph.D. Vol. I. 8vo, cloth, 21s.

*Swedenborg (Emanuel), Compendium of the Theological Writ-*ings of. 8vo, cloth, 9s.

Swedenborg (Emanuel): An Outline of his Life and Writings. By the Rev. John Hyde. Fifth Edition. Fcap. 8vo, cloth, 1s.

Swedenborg's Rules of Life. Beautifully illuminated, and printed on large card, 8d. each.

Swift, E., jun.—Manual of the Doctrines of the New Church. Third Edition. Fcap. 8vo, cloth gilt, 1s.

> *Emanuel Swedenborg; the Man and his Works.* Small crown 8vo, cloth, 2s. 6d.

Swift, Harold.—Heart Voices in Poetry and Prose. Small crown 8vo, cloth, 2s. 6d.

Tafel, Rev. Prof. R. L.—Documents concerning the Life and Character of Emanuel Swedenborg. Collected, translated, and annotated. 3 Vols. imperial 8vo, cloth, 30s.

   Authority in the New Church. Post 8vo, cloth, 4s. 6d.

Talks to the Children : Addresses delivered to the New Church Sunday School, Camden Road. Fcap. 8vo, cloth, 1s. 6d.

Tract-Sermons on New Church Principles without the Deno- minational Name. Cloth, 1s.

Ware, Mary G.—Thoughts in my Garden. Crown 8vo, cloth, 3s. 6d.

Warren, Miss L. E.—Birds of the Sacred Scriptures ; their Correspondence and Signification. Illustrated. Fcap. 8vo, cloth, 1s. 6d.

Wilkinson, J. J. Garth.—The Human Body, and its Connec- tion with Man. Crown 8vo, cloth, 5s.

   On Human Science, Good and Evil, and its Works ; and On Divine Revelation, and its Works and Sciences. 8vo, cloth, published at 16s., reduced to 8s.

Willie Harper's Two Lives : A Story for the Young. 18mo, sewed, 4d.

Words for the New Church. An Occasional Serial published by the Academy of the New Church in Philadelphia. Vols. I. and II., large 8vo, cloth, 8s. each.

PERIODICALS AND MAGAZINES.

Morning Light: A New Church Weekly				
Journal	.	.	.	. 8s. 8d. *per Annum.*
The New Church Magazine	.		. 6s. 0d.	,,
The Juvenile Magazine .		.	. 1s. 6d.	,,

The Works in this Catalogue are sent post or **carriage paid** to any part of the United Kingdom on receipt of the prices affixed.

Money Orders to be made payable at the Post Office, Great Russell Street, W.C.

NEW CHURCH TRACTS.

"The Lord He is God, and there is none else." By Rev. L. Noble. 1d.

Baptism: its Importance and Uses. By Rev. C. Giles. 1d.

The Essentials of Salvation: What are they? Do the Swedenborgians teach them? By Rev. W. Bates. 1d.

Who are these New Church People? to which is added A Week of Prayers. By Rev. Dr. Bayley. 1d.

A Truly Catholic Church: What are its Essential Principles? By Rev. C. Giles. 1d.

The Unity of God. By Rev. Dr. Bayley. 1d.

Jesus Christ the True and Only God. By James Spilling. 1d.

The Object for which Christ came into the World. By James Spilling. 1d.

The Second Coming of Christ. Christ is Coming, but how? By Rev. Dr. Bayley. 1d.

The Doctrines of the New Church the Measure of a Man. By Rev. C. Giles. 1d.

True Worship of the Lord: In what does it consist? By Rev. Prof. George Bush. 1d.

The True and Saving Faith. By James Spilling. 1d.

A Sermon on Leaves. By Rev. C. Giles. 1d.

Lecture on Swedenborg. By George Dawson. 1d.

The Annihilation Theory compared with Holy Scripture. By Rev. Joseph Deans. 1d.

The Resurrection: What it is, and when it takes place. By James Spilling. 1d.

Swedenborg. A Lecture. By J. W. Fletcher. 1d.

Perpetual Existence: A Discourse delivered before the House of Representatives at Washington. By Rev. Jabez Fox. 1d.

The Church of the New Jerusalem: A New Dispensation of Divine Truth. By Rev. C. Giles. 2d.

The Resurrection of Man. By Rev. C. Giles. 1d.

The Resurrection of the Lord. By Rev. C. Giles. 1d.

The Bible: Its Nature, and the Law of its Interpretation. By James Spilling. 1d.

"Thou shalt not:" Man's First Spiritual Duty. By Rev. C. Giles. 1d.

NEW CHURCH TRACTS.

The Doctrine of "Substitution" impartially examined. By Rev. J. Hyde. 1d.

The Servants of Sin. By Rev. C. Giles. 1d.

The Spiritual World the World of Life and Cause. By R. Jobson. 2d.

The Serpent that beguiled Eve. By Rev. J. Hyde. 1½d.

Take care of your Spiritual Bodies. By A. J. Johnson. 1d.

Christian Charity. By Rev. W. H. Mayhew. 1½d.

Doctrine: its Nature, its Use, and its Source. By Rev. W. H. Mayhew. 2d.

The New Church: its Spirit, Scope, and Purpose. By Rev. L. P. Mercer. 1d.

The Church of the New Jerusalem a Visible as well as a Universal New Church. By Rev. J. F. Potts, B.A. 1d.

The External of the Church as well as its Internal essential to its Existence. By Rev. J. F. Potts, B.A. 1d.

The Lord's Transfiguration. By Rev. C. Giles. 1d.

The Last Great Trumpet. By Rev. W. B. Hayden. 1d.

Worship: its Necessity, Nature, and Uses. By Rev. C. Giles. 1d.

The Daily Reading of a Portion of the Sacred Scripture. By James Speirs. 1d.

The Great Birthday. By James Speirs. 1d.

The Lord Jesus Christ the True Object of Christian Worship. By Rev. S. Noble. 2d.

That it is not so difficult to live the Life which leads to Heaven as is commonly supposed. By Emanuel Swedenborg. 1d.

Evolution and Natural Selection in the Light of the New Church. By E. Swift, jun. 1d.

Modern Spiritism in the Light of the New Church. By Rev. Prof. R. L. Tafel. 2d.

Our Children. By Rev. Prof. R. L. Tafel. 1d.

The Lord's Glorified Body. By Rev. Prof. R. L. Tafel. 2d.

The Feast of the Soul. By Rev. C. Giles. 1d.

Unfurnished Apartments. By Rev. J. Ashby. 1d.

The Nature and Use of the Memorable Relations. By Rev. C. Giles. 1d.

Spiritual House-Building. By Rev. C. Giles. 1d.

The Lilies of the Field. By Rev. C. Giles. 1d.

Anti-Mourning. A Lecture against the Unchristian Custom of wearing Mourning for the Dead. By Mrs. Hume-Rothery. 1d.

www.ingramcontent.com/pod-product-compliance
Lightning Source LLC
Chambersburg PA
CBHW020618030726
47497CB00007B/2308